## 'What the hell     you?'

Althea turned slowly from the window. Demos stood in the middle of the room; he'd shed his jacket and loosened his tie. He looked beautiful, virile, and utterly furious.

'Nothing's wrong with me,' she said slowly.

'You've been acting like a ghost since we married,' Demos accused. 'Did I marry a woman, Althea, or a shell?' He raked a hand through his hair.

'It's too late to back out now, if that's what you're thinking.'

'Yes, it's too late,' he agreed, his voice pitched low, a parody of pleasantness. 'No one's going to back out now.'

Althea knew what he meant. She'd been preparing for this moment. 'What are you saying?'

Demos's smile widened, although his eyes stayed hard and unforgiving. 'I want my wedding night.'

**Kate Hewitt** discovered her first Mills & Boon® romance on a trip to England when she was thirteen, and she's continued to read them ever since. She wrote her first story at the age of five, simply because her older brother had written one and she thought she could do it too. That story was one sentence long—fortunately they've become a bit more detailed as she's grown older. She has written plays, short stories, and magazine serials for many years, but writing romance remains her first love. Besides writing, she enjoys reading, travelling, and learning to knit.

After marrying the man of her dreams—her older brother's childhood friend—she lived in England for six years, and now resides in Connecticut with her husband, her three young children, and the possibility of one day getting a dog. Kate loves to hear from readers—you can contact her through her website, www.kate-hewitt.com

# THE GREEK TYCOON'S RELUCTANT BRIDE

BY
KATE HEWITT

⊚™ MILLS & BOON®
*Pure reading pleasure*™

First published in Great Britain 2008
Paperback edition 2009
Harlequin Mills & Boon Limited,
Eton House, 18-24 Paradise Road, Richmond, Surrey TW9 1SR

© Kate Hewitt 2008

ISBN: 978 0 263 86991 0

Set in Times Roman 10¼ on 11¼ pt
01-0109-54953

Printed and bound in Spain
by Litografia Rosés, S.A., Barcelona

# THE GREEK TYCOON'S RELUCTANT BRIDE

Dedicated to Lydia.
Thanks for being a great editor
and giving me a year of fantastic feedback
and support.
—K.

# PROLOGUE

'DO YOU need help?' Edward Jameson asked, pausing in the act of untying the rope that moored his yacht at Mikrolimano harbour. He raised one questioning eyebrow at the skinny determined boy standing by his boat.

'No.'

Edward pursed his lips and surveyed the still waiting boy-man in front of him. He couldn't be more than ten or twelve, and he looked like a scarecrow. His shirt and ragged trousers were too short for his long, scrawny arms and legs; it appeared he'd grown quickly and a lot. He also looked hungry, although from that determined glint in his silvery eyes he would never admit it.

'Do you want something, then?' Edward asked mildly. He spoke in Greek, for he doubted a Piraeus gutter rat like this one knew any other language. He looped the rope around one weathered wrist and waited.

The boy took a breath, puffing his thin chest out, and said, 'Actually, I was wondering the same thing about you.'

Edward let out a short admiring laugh. 'Were you?'

'Yes. I can do lots of things.' The boy spoke in a determined rush. 'I can wash your boat, carry messages, pump out the bilge water... I don't charge much.'

'Really?' He shook his head slowly. 'Shouldn't you be in school?'

Without a flicker of guilt or regret, the boy shrugged. 'I'm done with that.'

'How come?'

Another shrug, and this time there was a flicker of something... sorrow? Fear? 'I have a family to support.'

Edward choked back an incredulous laugh as he realised the boy was serious. 'What kind of family?'

'A mother and three sisters. The youngest is just a baby.' He folded his arms and gave Edward a level look. 'Now, are you going to hire me?'

There was no reason to hire a boy like this, Edward acknowledged. He was a millionaire, and he didn't need cheap labour—and inexperienced at that. Yet something in the boy's eyes—the utter determination to gain work, to survive—made him pause. 'Yes,' he said slowly, 'I believe I am.'

The boy allowed himself only a second's quick, triumphant grin before shoving his hands in his pockets and lifting his chin. 'When shall I start?'

'Does now suit you?' Edward asked, suspecting that it did.

'Sure. If you really need me.'

'I think I do. Tell me your name first, though.'

He threw his shoulders back. 'Demos Atrikes.' Edward gestured to him to come aboard, and nimbly, his eyes bright with anticipation, he did.

He stood in the centre of Edward's multimillion-pound yacht and only betrayed the level of his admiration by lightly touching the burnished wood of the railing, stroking it as if it were silk. Then he dropped his hand, tucking it back in the pocket of his trousers, and fixed Edward with a firm stare. 'What do you want me to do?'

'Tell me about your family first,' Edward said. 'Do you have to work so badly?'

Demos shrugged; no response was needed. It was, Edward thought sadly, all too apparent.

'They need me,' Demos said simply. 'So I'm here.'

Edward nodded. He knew what the choices were for a boy like this. The docks, the factories, or else the gangs. 'I need you to scrub the deck,' he finally said. 'I hope that's not too dirty a job for you?' he added, and Demos eyed him scornfully.

'I'll do anything,' he said, and Edward knew he meant it.

Edward watched as Demos set to scrubbing the deck, sluicing the boards with water and washing them with determined thoroughness. His shoulderblades poked through the back of his thin shirt like chicken wings, and the back of his neck burned red.

Edward worked him all day, knowing Demos would accept no less. When he finally presented him with a wad of drachma notes, Demos flicked through them with a hungry yet expert eye and nodded once.

'I'll be back tomorrow?' he said, and there was only a slight waver of uncertainty in his voice.

Edward nodded. 'Yes, I'm sure I'll need you then.' He'd think of something.

Demos nodded, and hopped easily off the yacht, walking barefoot down the dock, attracting a few irritated looks from the sleekly satisfied yachties. Yet he was utterly indifferent to their contempt.

Utterly above it.

On the cool, salt-tanged air Edward heard his jaunty whistling, and for a moment he looked like any other young Greek boy, loitering about the docks to gaze at the boats and have an afternoon's pleasure.

Then Edward's gaze drifted to the set of his shoulders, his ragged clothes, the drachma notes stuffed down his shirt where no one could steal them, and knew this boy was different.

He thought of the boy's words—*'I'll do anything'*—and wondered sadly if one day he would have to.

# CHAPTER ONE

*Twenty years later*

DEMOS ATRIKES lounged against a smooth stretch of wall and surveyed the strobe-lit dance floor with a jaundiced eye as music pounded and bodies writhed around him. Abstract images were projected on a rippling red curtain across from him, and the bored socialites who weren't on the dance floor lounged artfully on curving leather sofas, watching the absurd slideshow.

He already had a headache. He didn't normally come to these types of parties. Yet another striving socialite turning—what? Twenty-two? He glanced at the scantily clad beauties crowding the dance floor and suppressed a sigh of boredom. He generally preferred more sophisticated entertainments, although now even those had started to seem old. Empty.

He'd only come tonight because the birthday girl this time round also happened to be the daughter of one of his current clients, a financial analyst who wanted a custom-designed yacht, worth around twelve million euros.

It made coming to this pop princess party worth his while— or at least half an hour of his time. He downed the rest of his drink and surveyed the writhing crowd one last time. He'd had enough.

When he'd left the office half an hour ago he had been seeking respite, but he knew the pounding music and heaving dance floor would not provide it. He'd lost himself in such amusements too many times, and now he wanted something else. Something more.

He just didn't know what it was.

He'd begun to turn away when his eyes were drawn to a slender, dark-haired beauty in the middle of the floor, gyrating closely with a greasy-haired punk wearing tight black trousers and a half-buttoned silk shirt in a violent shade of pink. She wore a slip dress in silver-spangled Lycra, riding high on her thighs and dipping low on her breasts so that little of that lithe young body was left to Demos's imagination.

She smiled at the man next to her and he reached for her hips, drawing them closer to lock with his in a move so blatantly crude and sexual that Demos's mouth thinned in distaste— even though at thirty-two years old he wasn't old or innocent enough to be a prude.

His eyes flared with awareness and curiosity—blatant interest—uncoiled inside him as he watched the girl stiffen. Was the punk's proprietorial pawing too much, even for a wild-child like her? Then she shrugged, accepting, and tossed back her tangled waves of ink-black hair in a gesture that was both brave and yet somehow wonderfully, pitiably defiant.

They danced like that for a few seconds, no more, before she suddenly twisted away, her hair lashing around her, and moved off the dance floor.

Demos watched, intrigued, as the man in the lurid shirt made to follow her. But with a flirty smile that managed to both promise and reject she shook her head and disappeared among the heated throng.

Without even thinking about what he was doing—or why— Demos followed.

It didn't take long to find her. At six feet four he was head and shoulders above all the women, even those tottering on their sharpened stilettos, and most of the men.

He found her curled up on one of the curving divans scattered around the nightclub's bar area, her eyes wide and staring. Demos stopped and watched her, considering his move.

He hadn't been in the mood to party tonight, he acknowledged, not after nine hours of staring at blueprints, followed by his mother's reproachful telephone call. *You must visit, Demos. Your sisters need you...*

A mantle, a yoke he'd taken on without a qualm or single pang of uncertainty. Yet now, twenty years later, he felt its shackling weight.

For a moment he threw it off, let his gaze rest on a far more enticing proposition—someone who didn't depend on him, didn't need him, someone he just...wanted. Desire. Pure, plain, simple.

He wanted her. Yet she was oblivious to his presence even though he'd come to a halt only a metre away. He took the opportunity to study her: the sexily tousled hair, the smoky eyeliner and pink pouty lips, the distant look in eyes the colour of lapis-lazuli. She was sitting with her legs tucked under her, and her minuscule skirt rode up even higher so he could see the scrap of her thong.

As if aware of where his wandering eyes had strayed, she snapped her own gaze to his, and for a heartbeat she looked surprised—shocked, even. Demos held her gaze, felt its lure and promise as those pouty lips curved into a smile of sensual enjoyment and with deliberate provocation she recrossed her legs.

Demos swallowed, not wanting to be affected by such an obvious ploy. But he was. Her lips curved more deeply, knowingly.

'Had a nice look?' she asked in a husky purr, and Demos smiled, slipping next to her on the divan.

'Yes,' he murmured back, 'thanks to you.'

She glanced at him with brazen thoroughness, her gaze travelling from his face, with its five o'clock shadow, down to his loosened tie, sweeping across his chest, and down further, her smile still curving with a teasing playfulness that had Demos nearly breaking into a sweat.

He'd had his share of one-night stands—instant physical attraction that had been fulfilled and finished in a matter of moments. Yet he'd never reacted so strongly, so quickly, to a simple look.

'Had a good look yourself?' he asked, leaning closer to her. She shook her head, and her hair brushed his cheek. She smelled of some kind of flowery young scent that he normally would have found overpowering, yet on her it was intoxicating.

'No…not yet.'

'We could remedy that situation.'

She pulled back, raised her eyebrows. 'How?'

She was challenging him, he thought. The smile that curved her lips was both sensual and mocking. He felt a thrill of adrenalin and lust race through him. This girl was different from the spoiled socialites, the shallow models. The women he normally took to bed.

They simpered, they cooed, they draped themselves over him with nauseating predictability. She didn't. She just smiled coolly and waited.

'How do you think?' he finally asked.

'I don't know,' she replied, and he felt from her little smile that she was as intrigued as he was. 'Maybe you can make some suggestions as to how we find out.' There was a look of challenge in her eyes, and she laid one hand as lightly as a butterfly's wing on his thigh. High on his thigh.

And Demos reacted.

So did she.

She jerked her hand away and gave a little laugh, her glance sliding away from his before it returned, resolutely, to meet his enquiring gaze.

The skinny silver strap of her dress had fallen off her shoulder, and Demos reached to adjust it. He couldn't resist sweeping his fingers against that silky bit of skin, to feel if it was as soft as it looked.

Yet the moment his fingers skimmed her collarbone she

jerked back, her body stiffening, her eyes blanking. She almost looked afraid.

Demos dropped his hand and leaned back, considering.

What game was she playing?

Then she smiled again, reached for her martini glass, downed the last of her drink and thrust it towards him.

'Why don't we start with you buying me a drink?'

Althea Paranoussis held her glass out, quirking one eyebrow in mocking challenge. The man next to her stared at her for a moment, his own eyes the colour of smoke, darkening to charcoal.

Hard eyes, she thought. Hard mouth, hard face, hard body. Hard everything. She didn't like the cool assessment in his eyes, the way his long fingers wrapped around her glass, taking care to brush hers.

She didn't like the shock of pure sensation that shot up her arm, uncoiled in her belly and put the familiar metallic tang of fear on her tongue.

'What are you drinking?' he asked.

She told him the cocktail she wanted. A name laced with innuendo.

He raised his eyes, and Althea flicked her hair over her shoulders in a move she'd perfected over the years.

'Is that a drink?'

'You'll find out at the bar,' she replied with a naughty little smile.

He gave a terse nod and moved from the divan. Althea watched his long, lean body as it moved through the crowds with easy grace. As he headed towards the bar she wondered if she should disappear.

She was an expert at the art of promising without delivering, of melting into the crowd as she made a little moue of regret. It was the way she stayed safe. Sane.

She leaned back against the leather divan and didn't move. She wanted to see him again, she realised with a sharp pang of surprise. That was strange. She wanted to know more about him. He seemed different from the bored, base young men she normally surrounded herself with. He was older, more confident, and therefore more dangerous. Yet still she didn't move.

There would be time later for excuses, escapes.

Plenty of time.

She glanced up and saw he'd already reappeared, requisite pink drink in hand. It was a ridiculous drink, a silly, soppy, girly cocktail, and she swallowed a laugh at the look of it in his hand. He looked revolted by it, but he handed it to her with a flourish, and the laugh she'd suppressed came out in a rich, throaty chuckle that had him smiling back in bemusement as well as blatant appreciation.

'Perfect,' she murmured. He hadn't bought a drink for himself, Althea noticed as she took a small, careful sip.

He sat down next to her, watching her with an intent narrowed gaze that lacked the lascivious speculation she was used to and yet affected her more deeply, causing a strange shaft of pleasure and pain to pierce her composure, her armour, as his eyes swept slowly over her.

'I don't even know your name.'

She smiled over the rim of her glass and sought to arm herself once more. 'Maybe it's better that way.'

He raised an eyebrow. 'Is that how you like it?'

'Sometimes,' she shot back carelessly. She put her drink down, not quite meeting his eyes.

'I like women to know *my* name,' he replied. His eyes glinted with both challenge and admiration. 'Demos Atrikes,' he said after a moment, and she tossed her hair back and smiled.

'Pleased to meet you.' She'd heard of him, of course. She supposed she should have recognised him. He was in the tabloids just as much she was, usually with a model or starlet clinging to his arm. And now he wanted her for that precarious position.

Her lips thinned before she smiled again, letting her gaze linger on the harsh yet beautiful lines of his face, noticing the gold flecks in his silver-grey eyes. Silver and gold. The man was rich, she knew. Rich and bored, out for an evening's entertainment. She leaned back against the leather divan, tucking her legs under her, her mouth twisting sardonically.

He noticed. 'Something wrong?' he asked in a murmur, his voice pitched low yet sharpened with cynicism.

'I'm bored.' Althea met his gaze with a challenge of her own. 'Let's dance.'

'You bore easily.'

'Not if given the right entertainment,' she tossed back, eyes and senses flaring.

'I have a better idea,' Demos murmured, leaning towards her so she could feel his breath, cool and minty on her cheek. 'Let's leave this party. I know a taverna near here. We can have a drink, some quiet conversation.'

Althea pulled back, raised one eyebrow in mocking disbelief. 'You want to *talk*?'

'We can begin with talking,' Demos replied with a smile. 'And see where it leads.' He paused, his eyes flickering over her once again. 'You're different.'

She smiled again, not bothering to hide her cynicism. He had no idea how *different* she was. 'I'll take that as a compliment.'

'It was intended as one. So?' Demos arched an eyebrow, his eyes dark with enquiry and interest. 'Shall we?'

She shouldn't. She knew she shouldn't. She didn't get that close with men like Demos Atrikes. She didn't get them alone.

Yet she was intrigued despite her intentions not to be, despite her *self*. He had told her she was different, and now she wondered if he really was too.

It was more than simple curiosity, Althea knew. Her eyes were drawn to the hand he extended, lean and brown and sure. She wondered how that hand would feel wrapped around hers, how his body, lean and long and hard, would feel against hers, and the very fact that she was wondering such things made her breathless and dizzy with fearful surprise.

Althea felt herself slip from the divan even as a discon-nected voice reminded her that she *never* did this. He was just a man, another man, and she *knew*...

Except maybe she didn't know. Maybe she wanted to find out. She tossed her hair back and reached for the scrap of spangled silk that served as a wrap. Even in Athens the early spring air was chilly. It had a bite.

She slipped her hand in his and felt those strong brown fingers close around hers, sending a jolt of pure sensation through her like a shot to the heart. It wasn't a pleasant feeling; it was too strong and surprising. Althea jerked back, but Demos didn't let go.

He just smiled, and Althea realised he'd sensed her reaction and knew what it meant. Maybe he felt it too.

Out of the corner of her eye she saw a glint of pink silk, and her stomach curled with nerves as Angelos Fotopolous walked straight towards her, smiling with unpleasant promise. She turned back to Demos.

'Come on, let's go.'

'In a hurry, are you?' he murmured, even as Althea rested a hand on his arm, her fingers curling, clinging to his suit jacket.

'You're not leaving the party so soon, beautiful?' Angelos said. He'd undone a further button on his shirt and his hair was slicked back from his narrow face.

He reached out to pull her to him, and Althea let herself go slack, unresisting. She felt her body go numb, and then... nothing.

He didn't touch her.

Demos had stopped that snaking arm with a quick vice-like grip. 'She's leaving,' he said in a low, pleasant voice. 'With me.'

'Says who?' Angelos snarled, yet Althea saw the uncertainty enter his eyes. Demos was a head taller and a decade older than Angelos, who still had a rime of pimples along his jaw.

'She says,' Demos replied. 'Don't you?' he asked, sliding her a quick querying glance. He was, she realised, giving her a choice. She hadn't expected it. She had expected him to defend her against Angelos as a matter of personal pride. But to let her choose…? It was novel.

Maybe he *was* different.

'I…' She cleared her throat, raised her voice. 'I do. Leave it, Angelos.'

Angelos's eyes blazed, but he shrugged. 'Fine. She's nothing but an easy slut anyway.'

Demos's hand shot out, wrapped around Angelos's throat. Althea blinked. Angelos choked.

'Apologise, please,' Demos said. His eyes were hard, almost black, even though he kept his voice pleasant.

'You'll find out soon enough,' Angelos gasped, his fingers scrabbling at Demos's fist. Speculative murmurs rippled around them in an uneasy tide. They were, Althea realised, attracting a crowd.

'Demos—enough,' she said. She lifted her shoulder in a dismissive shrug. 'He's not worth it.'

Demos waited a few seconds, watched as Angelos's face began to turn colour. Then he let him go. 'No, he's not,' he agreed with an unpleasant little smile. He stepped away. 'Let's go.'

Demos turned his back on Angelos and his arm, heavy, guiding, went around Althea's shoulders. She tensed as he led her through the curious throng, the crowd parting easily and quickly for a man of Demos's size and presence.

Within seconds they were on the street outside the club— little more than a narrow alleyway in the city's Psiri district.

'I know a place near here,' Demos said, and with his arm still around her shoulders he began striding down the street.

Although the district was a working class neighbourhood of small shops and factories during the day, at night the tavernas and ouzeries opened up, spilling their tables and patrons out onto the street along with raucous laughter and the twangy strains of old *rembetika* songs.

High-profile nightclubs had attracted Athens's A-List, but

now Demos was leading her to another part of Psiri altogether; a part, Althea thought with a shiver, that reminded her of the district's origins in revolutionaries and organised crime.

'Where are we going?' she asked, and Demos flashed her a quick smile, his teeth gleaming in the darkness.

The pounding music and pulsing lights of the club were far behind, and somewhere in the darkness a wild cat yowled.

'Don't worry,' Demos said, but Althea jerked away from him.

'I want to know where we're going.' She wrapped her arms around herself, suddenly conscious of how skimpy her attire really was. In the crowd of a club it felt appropriate. Here, alone with Demos on an empty darkened street, it felt ridiculous, dangerous. And freezing.

She was also conscious of how little she knew Demos; she'd been intrigued in the club—excited, even—yet now fear, cold and familiar, came rushing back.

Demos regarded her for a moment, and in the yellow wash of a passing car's headlights Althea could see a considering gleam in his eyes. 'There's a little taverna on the next street,' he said. 'A quiet place, with good wine.'

Althea took a breath, tried not to think of the implications of his invitation. She made it a policy never to get this far, this *close*. Yet she'd broken that cardinal rule, and now she didn't know what to do. How to act.

He'd led her through a maze of twisting alleys and streets and she had no idea how to get back to the club, or even to a thoroughfare that would have reliable taxis. She nodded slowly, and then forced herself to shrug. 'Fine.'

He held out his hand, and with another shrug and a little smile Althea took it. She shouldn't like the way his hand felt encasing hers, she knew, warm and dry and safe. She shouldn't curl her fingers around his as if she wanted him to keep holding her, touching her. Yet she did.

A few minutes later they arrived at the promised taverna, a narrow, quaint place, crammed with tables and rickety chairs, dusty bottles lining the walls. The proprietor, a tall, gangling man in a three-piece suit and apron, welcomed them in.

'Demos! Long time, eh? What brings you here?'

'A party,' Demos said with a shrug, but he clapped the man on the shoulder and smiled. 'Good to see you, Andreolos.'

Althea was surprised. From the innate grace and arrogance with which he'd strode through the club, not to mention dealt with Angelos, she'd expected him to entertain at five-star hotels on the Plaka, not dusty holes-in-the-wall in Psiri.

Andreolos ushered them to a table tucked in the corner, gave them menus and went to fetch a bottle of wine from under the bar. Althea wrapped her spangled shawl more modestly around herself, conscious yet again of how tarty she must appear.

'Regretting your choice of attire?' Demos asked, and she heard a mocking note in his voice that made her flush. Then he surprised her by adding quietly, 'You look beautiful.'

In the dim intimacy of the taverna, with their knees touching under the tiny table, she took a moment to study the man whose attention and interest she'd captured. And had he captured hers? She considered the question reluctantly; she didn't like to think that a man—any man—could have a hold over any part of her. Body, mind, heart.

Yet she'd gone with him; she'd been planning to go with him even before Angelos had intercepted their exit. She'd *wanted* to.

Why?

She thought of that deep shaft of pleasure-pain she'd felt when he looked at her, touched her, and then shoved the memory away with resolute determination.

She couldn't afford memories like that.

He glanced down at the laminated menu, giving her ample time to study his features.

He was good-looking, undoubtedly, although not in the stylised, almost feminine way most of the young men of her circle were.

His face wasn't beautiful; it was too rugged and individual

for that. His hair was dark, longer than most men's, touching his collar, raked arrogantly back from his face. His eyes were silvery grey under fierce arching brows. His nose would have been straight and perfect if not for a slight crook in the middle, suggesting it had been broken at some time in the distant past. And his mouth…lips that were sculpted, full. Surprisingly soft in such a hard face.

She tried to remember what the tabloids said about him, but the details escaped her. She tried never to read the gossip rags anyway. She knew all too well how they twisted the truth and lied outright. And she let them.

Andreolos came with the bottle of wine and two glasses, and they were both silent as he poured. Demos smiled his thanks at the man, then lifted his glass in a toast, the ruby-coloured liquid glinting in the lamplight.

'*Yasas*,' he said, in the familiar drinking toast, and Althea murmured it back before she took a sip. 'So,' he said musingly, and Althea tensed. 'Tell me about yourself.'

She took another sip of wine. 'What do you want to know?'

'Your name, to start.'

Althea smiled mischievously. 'I thought we agreed it would be better if you didn't know.'

His mouth quirked in an answering smile. 'Woman of mystery?'

'Of course.'

He chuckled, and Althea wondered why it mattered. It didn't make sense; he could find her name out easily enough by asking anyone in that club. She was surprised that he didn't know it already, and that she'd never seen him outside the tabloids before.

She noticed now a few grey streaks at his temples, and wondered how old he was. Older than most of her crowd, at any rate. Older and more experienced—more sophisticated. More dangerous, she reminded herself.

She took another sip of wine.

'All right, Woman of Mystery,' Demos said, his tone lazy and languorous, 'I suppose I'll have to think of a name for you myself.'

Althea's lips curved. 'Such as?'

He studied her, his eyes heavy-lidded over the rim of his wine glass. 'Elpis,' he finally said at last, and Althea let out a short laugh of disbelief.

'That's an interesting choice.'

'Do you know who she is?'

'Yes, as a matter of fact I do.' Her eyes flashed. 'Hope. The only thing left in Pandora's box.' She quirked an eyebrow. 'Do you know who *she* is?'

He laughed, and she could tell he had recognised how he'd patronised her. 'Vaguely,' he admitted, his eyes glinting in the dim light, sending a strange shiver of foreboding through Althea. She shouldn't let him affect her like this…even if he was different.

'So.' She placed her wine glass on the table and leaned forward, her wrap slipping off one shoulder. 'What kind of hope do I give you?' she asked, and there was a knowing, sardonic edge to her voice that had his eyebrows rising in surprise.

His eyes flicked over her, resting briefly on her bare shoulder. 'I think you know,' he murmured.

She smiled, leaned back, and said nothing. She felt the slight, stupid sting of disappointment. It was about sex. Always about sex. Just sex. *Of course.* Had she thought for a moment he wanted something more? Had she hoped for it? *Why?*

Maybe he wasn't so different after all.

'So tell me about yourself,' she said after a moment. Demos shrugged.

'I'm a yacht designer. I also run a business letting luxury yachts to the discerning customer.' He smiled and she nodded, her interest piqued. He wasn't another boy intent on spending his father's inheritance. He was a man who had presumably made his own money.

'You like it?' she asked.

'Very much.'

'Why?'

The question surprised him, she could tell. He took a sip of wine before speaking. 'I like to see the designs come to life. From nothing, to lines on paper, to something made of steel and glass—something that races across the sea.' He gave a little smile, almost of embarrassment, as if he'd said too much.

'That must be a nice feeling,' Althea agreed, and she couldn't quite keep the wistful note from her voice. 'To create something.'

'And what do you do? Besides play and party.'

She raised her eyebrows. 'Do I need to do anything else?'

'A beautiful woman need only exist,' Demos replied smoothly. Too smoothly.

'An ornament, you mean?' Althea said flatly, and she could tell he was surprised. He thought he'd been complimenting her.

'So tell me what you do, then,' he said, a cool note entering his voice.

Althea smiled sardonically, although she kept her voice light. 'I exist, of course.' Exist. So much less than living, loving. Nothing more than a state of being.

She could feel Demos's eyes on her—felt his curiosity, his interest and, worse, a flicker of compassion. Pity.

'Are you happy?' he asked, and Althea realised no one had ever asked that before.

She looked up, saw him smile and laughed—a hard, brittle sound. 'Of course I am. Look at me.' She raised her arms. 'Do you honestly think a woman like me could be unhappy?'

It was a bold question, one she didn't want answered. She was beautiful; she knew that. Beautiful people didn't have problems. Beautiful people were always happy. They had to be.

Demos's gaze moved over her slowly, thoughtfully. Althea watched and waited. She wanted to look away; she wanted to hide. She hated feeling examined, explained away, yet for some reason Demos didn't look like a man trying to find answers. He looked more in search of questions. 'I would find it difficult to believe,' he finally said, and Althea dropped her arms.

'There you are, then,' she said, and drained her glass.

The ensuing silence hummed and buzzed between them with expectation, and Althea toyed with the stem of her wine glass. 'Are you married?' she asked after a moment.

Demos's own glass slammed onto the table with enough force to send liquid sloshing over the rim. Andreolos hurried forward and dabbed at the spill before retiring once more.

'What the hell kind of question is that?'

Althea shrugged. 'I have to ask.'

'Do married men pick you up in clubs often?' he asked, and she wondered if the distaste thickening his tone was for her or for the married men.

'I try to stay away from wedding rings,' she replied.

Demos arched one eyebrow. 'Even on your own finger?'

'Absolutely.'

He paused, his eyes hard and bright with speculative satisfaction. 'Then we shouldn't have a problem.'

He smiled, and she watched as he poured her more wine. No problem, she thought, because he had no intention of marrying. No intention, perhaps, of even calling her or seeing her again. A few preliminaries, the standard 'tell me about yourself', and then his undoubtedly well-used one-liner about Pandora's box. *Hope*.

For heaven's sake. She'd almost fallen for it, almost wondered—believed—that he was different.

That *she* was.

Althea closed her eyes briefly; she felt a sudden sorrowful weariness that threatened to wash over her in an endless tide. She was so tired of men like Demos. So tired of nights like this. So tired of being the party princess who never said no to a drink, a dance.

Who didn't know how.

She opened her eyes and saw Demos looking at her with far too much perception—and yet not nearly enough. Had she thought he might understand? Might *want* to? Was that why she'd come out with him alone, unescorted, unprotected? Dancing in a club was safe. Flirting, partying, promising. All safe.

This wasn't.

She needed safety. She needed escape. She needed it now.

She flicked her hair back with a little smile, her decision made. 'Where's the ladies' room in a place like this?'

'It's a closet in the back,' Demos replied. His eyes narrowed slightly as he added, 'Probably not what you're used to.'

'Not to worry.' Althea slid from her chair, taking her wrap and her tiny beaded bag, trying to act casual. Her heart was starting to thump so loudly she was sure Demos could hear it, see it through her skimpy dress. 'Be back in a moment,' she promised with a little smile, and he nodded.

She wove her way through the tables, down a narrow corridor to the bathroom at the back. She could see a few men in greasy aprons cooking in the tiny kitchen at the end of the hallway. They glanced up as she approached, then turned back to their flaming skillets. There was a door, she saw with relief, to a back courtyard.

She waited a moment, until she couldn't see anyone either in front or behind, and then strode quickly to the back door. For a second, no more, she imagined turning around and going back to the table. Sitting with Demos, drinking good wine, talking, laughing, learning about each other.

And where would it lead? Where would he expect it to lead? Where did he intend for it to lead? He'd already told her. Hope.

*Ha.*

With a grim little smile she clenched the knob and wrenched the door open. Outside in the cramped courtyard she breathed in a lungful of greasy fumes; the vent from the kitchen blew out into the cluttered space. There was an overflowing skip of rubbish next to the door, a couple of rickety chairs, no doubt placed for the waiters to have their cigarette breaks, and high, soot-stained stone walls separating the courtyard from those of the neighbouring buildings. On every side.

There was no way out.

Althea slowly circled the courtyard before cursing aloud. She was trapped.

'Going somewhere, Elpis?'

Her breath came out in a startled rush and her eyes flew to Demos, now lounging in the doorway, a sardonic smile curving that mobile mouth, his eyes glinting in the darkness. He looked lazily amused, yet underneath Althea sensed something deeper, darker.

She swallowed and opened her mouth, but couldn't think of a single thing to say. The evidence was obvious. Impossible to deny. She'd been trying to run out on him.

He uncoiled himself from his relaxed pose and closed the space between them in a couple of strides.

'I don't think you were skipping out on the bill,' he murmured, though she heard the edge in his voice. Felt it. He was close enough that his breath ruffled her hair. 'So you must have been skipping out on me.' He tucked a strand of hair behind her ear and Althea shivered. 'And I'm wondering why.'

He stood so close to her she could feel his heat. She felt her mind go numb. Blank.

'Cold feet?' he whispered against her hair, mockery hardening his tone. 'Or are you just playing a game?'

Althea was tall, but she still wasn't at eye-level with him. She stared straight ahead at the collar of his shirt, opened at the throat, saw the sharp line of his collarbone, the skin tanned a deep, working man's brown. She swallowed and said nothing.

Demos lifted his hand, trailed his fingers lightly down her cheek. 'You intrigue me, Elpis,' he whispered. 'You're differ-

nt from most of the spoiled socialites I meet. I think you might
e as bored with the club scene as I am.' She arced her head
way from him, and his fingers closed around her chin, tilting
t so she was forced to meet his iron gaze. 'But I don't play
ames, so you'd better not try them with me.'

Something sparked to life and she jerked her chin from his
rip. 'All of this is a game.'

'Is it?' His eyes fastened on hers, searching, demanding.
And who wins, I wonder?'

Althea's lips curved in a smile. Her heart was pounding so
ard she felt sick. She shook her hair back, smiled again. She
et the smile play about her lips, let Demos notice, saw his own
yes darken with desire even as his mouth remained unsmiling
nd hard. 'And the game is over, Demos,' she whispered. 'For
onight. If I intrigue you so much you'll have to work a little
arder. Find out my name first…and it's not Elpis.' Then, driven
y a need she couldn't even name, she stood on her tiptoes and
eaned forward, meaning only to brush her lips with his in the
arest kiss of farewell.

She planned on never seeing him again. Certainly not alone.

Demos stilled her, his hands curling around her shoulders.
'heir lips were a breath apart. 'Are you sure this is how you
vant to end tonight?' he asked in a lazy murmur, and Althea
elt control trickling away, felt her body and mind freeze once
nore. 'Because,' Demos continued, 'I've been wondering what
t will feel like to kiss you all evening. What you taste like. And
think you've been wondering the same thing.'

She couldn't open her mouth to deny it; his lips were too close.

'And I think,' Demos continued with a knowing edge, his lips
lmost—*almost*—brushing hers as he spoke, 'I'm going to let
ou wonder a little bit more. You want me, Elpis. You want me
s much as I want you. I can tell.'

Althea wanted to tell him to go to hell. She wanted to deny
t with as much scathing disdain as she could muster. And yet
he couldn't quite make herself say the words.

She'd never wanted anyone. Any man. And she sure as he[
wouldn't want this arrogant ass either.

Demos's mouth hovered over hers a second longer, lon[
enough for Althea's lips to part in instinctive invitation, eve[
though her mind was screaming its useless denial. She felt hi[
smile against her mouth, and then he stepped back an[
released her.

'I'll get you a taxi.'

For a shattered second all Althea could do was stare, blin[
her mind and body shocked and numb. Then she nodde[
mutely, still unable to form a thought, much less a sound. Sh[
knew it would be difficult for her to get a taxi in this part [
Psiri—a woman alone on the street. And she wanted to g[
home…alone. Even if Demos had won this round. Even if sh[
was left wondering, wanting, unsure and unsated.

She followed Demos through the taverna, weaving her wa[
through the tables, and tried to ignore Andreolos and the oth[
waiters' speculative looks.

Out in the street a couple staggered past them, laughing u[
roariously and clearly drunk.

Althea wrapped her arms around herself. The wind ha[
picked up and was now slicing through her skimpy dress.

Demos hailed a taxi in a matter of seconds—an admirab[
accomplishment in any part of Athens, and certainly in th[
neighbourhood.

Althea pushed past him without a word, too frozen in bod[
and spirit even to offer her thanks. She felt something heav[
drop over her shoulders and she stiffened in surprise.

It was his blazer.

'You're shivering,' he said, and handed the taxi driver [
wad of euros.

'I don't—'

'Yes,' he replied with flat certainty, 'you do.' He closed th[
door in her face, leaving her alone in the darkened tax[
speeding away, his jacket still on her shoulders.

* * *

Demos watched the taxi disappear around the corner and wondered where she was going. He wondered who she was.

He was intrigued by her spirit, her *sass*, as well as by the hidden depths in those jewel-like eyes. She wasn't, he mused, an empty-headed socialite—even though she pretended to be one. He had a feeling she wasn't the easy slut Angelos had claimed her to be either.

So who was she? And why did he want her so much?

Was it the challenge, the mystery? Or the simple fact that he was currently unattached and bored?

No, it had to be more than that; there had been at least a dozen debutantes in that forsaken club that would have gladly come home with him. He hadn't given them a single look. They hadn't been worth a single thought.

But her...

She'd been going to run out on him. He smiled at her sheer audacity and nerve, even though he'd been furious—furious and stupidly a little hurt—at the time.

Why had she been sneaking out? Had she been bored? Provocative? Or something else altogether? He didn't like games. He should have left her there—alone, humiliated. Yet he hadn't. He couldn't have.

She had courage. She was beautiful. He wanted her.

Three reasons to make her his, however he could. But first he needed a name.

It didn't take long. Nothing ever did when you had determination. Demos had discovered that long ago. He paid the bouncer at the club fifty euros to find Angelos and bring him outside.

Demos leaned against the graffiti-splattered brick wall as Angelos came out, looking surly and suspicious.

'You...!' he said in disbelief, and then looked quickly around, noticing that the bouncer had stepped closely behind him. 'What do you want?'

'A name.'

* * *

Angelos shook his head, nonplussed and not a little drunk 'What?'

'The name,' Demos repeated softly, 'of the woman I wa with tonight.'

Angelos snorted. 'You didn't even get her *name*?' He glance around, saw that Althea was absent. 'She tired of you quick hey? She'll come running to me. Althea and I go way back.'

'Althea,' Demos repeated in satisfaction. It suited her.

'Althea Paranoussis,' Angelos confirmed with a shrug 'Daddy's little rich girl. Stupid sl—'

'Don't,' Demos warned him. 'Don't speak of her again. Ever

'What do you care?' Angelos took a step backwards, and cam up against the bouncer. 'She left you anyway. She's good at that

'I'm finished here.' Demos addressed the bouncer, the started down the street. He didn't look back as Angelos wa hustled into the club.

Althea Paranoussis. He had a name. He knew how to fin her. And he would, Demos thought with satisfaction. Soon.

# CHAPTER TWO

SUNLIGHT poured through the wide windows of Althea's bedroom, touching the single bed and the girlish white bureau with gold.

Althea lay flat on her back, unmoving, her eyes focused on the blank ceiling. She heard the deliberate heavy tread of her father down the front stairs of their town house and knew he was up, early as always, ready to take a cup of black tea and a *koulourakia* in the dining room, as he'd done every day of his adult life.

Althea let her breath out slowly but still did not move. She wondered if her father was still angry about her return last night. She hadn't been out all that late, but he'd clearly been waiting for her to come home, and every second so spent had strained his patience.

He was tired of her. Tired of her parties, her late nights, her increasingly wild reputation. Althea smiled grimly. She was tired too.

'This has to stop, Althea,' Spiros Paranoussis had said last night. He'd been in his pyjamas and dressing gown, his white hair thin and wispy, his face flushed with anger. 'You stop this behaviour or I shall have to stop it myself.'

'I'm a grown woman, Father,' Althea replied coolly. She'd stopped calling him Papa when she was twelve.

'Acting like a spoiled child! Every day there is another story in the tabloids about what you've done, who you've been with. How am I to hold my head up in town? At work?'

Althea shrugged. 'That's not my concern.'

'It is, alas, mine,' Spiros said coldly. 'And if you cannot see fit to curb your behaviour then I shall have to do so for you...by whatever means necessary.'

Althea had shrugged again and gone upstairs. He'd been threatening her for years with consequences he never cared to enforce. She refused to take her father seriously, refused to grant him the respect he demanded—the respect he felt he deserved—and it infuriated him. But he'd lost the right to her respect too many years ago for her to even consider giving it to him now.

With another sigh Althea swung her legs out of bed. She felt woozy, even though she hadn't had much to drink last night. Just the cocktail and the glass of wine provided by Demos.

Demos... The mere thought of him caused her to wrap her arms around herself in a movement guided by self-protection. Safety.

He'd affected her too much. Made her think, made her feel, and she didn't want to do either. She thought of the way his lips had almost—*almost*—brushed hers last night, and even now a deep stabbing shaft of need made her realise she'd wanted his kiss.

She still did.

With a sigh she pushed her hair from her face and gazed dispiritedly at her reflection in the mirror. She was pale—too pale. The freckles were standing out on her cheeks and nose, her eyes burning bright and blue, and her hair a tangled mass pushed carelessly away from her face. She looked like the unruly child her father had accused her of being last night.

Althea's mouth twisted. Yet what recourse did she have? Living in her father's house, a high school drop-out, with no education, no money, no hope.

Hope.

Elpis.

He'd never been so far from the truth.

She slipped into a pair of skinny jeans and a close-fitting cashmere sweater in a soft, comforting grey, then tied her hair back with a scarf and slapped on a bit of make-up.

As she left the room she paused by the blazer she'd slung on a low settee. Against her better judgement she picked it up and held it to her face. It smelled of the nightclub, of stale cigarette smoke and cheap beer. But underneath those familiar and unpalatable scents was something deeper, foreign yet intimate. Demos.

She breathed in the tang of brine mixed with the clean scent of a woodsy aftershave. After a second's hesitation she felt the pockets, but they were empty. Her lips curved in a reluctant smile; she had no doubt this was intentional. Demos Atrikes was going to find her, not the other way round.

And did she want to be found? Pushing the question as well as the unformed answer away, she left her bedroom.

Downstairs the housekeeper, Melina, was arranging a display of purple asters in a vase in the foyer. She gave Althea a sorrowful look and shook her head. 'What have you done to make your papa so cross?'

Althea smiled thinly. 'Nothing more than usual.'

Melina frowned, turning back to the flowers. 'You were a good girl once,' she said, which was her standard protest.

'People change,' Althea replied, with a deliberately wicked little laugh, and Melina's frown deepened.

'You need to be good to him. He works hard for you.'

'And for himself,' Althea replied, but she softened this reply by kissing the older woman's wrinkled cheek. 'Don't fuss at me this early in the day, Melina.'

Melina sighed, and Althea moved past her into the kitchen. She liked Melina, yet she'd long ago recognised how much the housekeeper was capable of. These mild, ineffectual protests were the extent of her involvement in the family's affairs.

Althea paused on the threshold of the dining room. Her father sat rigidly at the head of the table, a teacup halfway to his lips. He didn't turn as he said, 'Althea. Are you joining me for breakfast?'

She hadn't eaten a meal with him in months. 'No, I'm going out.'

Spiros bristled. 'Where, may I ask?'

'Shopping.'

'You need more clothes?' He turned slightly, and Althea saw his eyebrows rise haughtily. He was a banker and a millionaire, but he had always been tight-fisted.

'As a matter of fact, no. But my friend seems to think she does, and I'm going with her.' Althea made to leave.

'When will you return?'

She turned back and saw the faint look of bewilderment on her father's face, as if he couldn't understand how they had come to this, descended to this. When she was little he'd taken her to the seaside, bought her ice creams, tucked her in bed. He looked at her now as if he wanted to know why that adorable little girl had become this defiant young woman. Yet he couldn't quite bring himself to ask the question.

And Althea would never bring herself to answer it.

That confused, saddened look had used to soften her, but now it only disgusted her, moved her to contempt rather than compassion.

She shook her head, her eyes hard.

'Later.' Without another word she left the townhouse.

The sunlight sparkled on the placid water of the marina at Mikrolimano as humble fishing boats and luxurious yachts bobbed next to each other against a vista of whitewashed apartments and shops.

It was morning, but the sun was hot on the deck of Edward Jameson's yacht as Demos stretched his legs out and took a sip of strong black coffee. 'Tell me what you know of Spiro Paranoussis.'

Across the table Edward Jameson cut his fried egg into precise squares. Even though he spent half a year on his yacht in various European harbours, he still insisted on a full English breakfast to start his morning. Now he looked up, raising his eyebrows. Underneath shaggy white brows his pale blue eyes glinted shrewdly, full of easy humour.

'Spiros Paranoussis? Why should I know anything of him at all?'

Demos smiled and shrugged. 'Because I know enough to know he's a banker in Athens, and you know everyone in finance in this city—as well as in most others in Europe.'

Edward smiled faintly and inclined his head. 'Spiros Paranoussis…' he mused. 'Yes, he's a banker. Second generation, current CEO of Attica Finance. Solid businessman, although rather uninspired. He hasn't made much money, but he's kept what he has.'

Demos nodded thoughtfully, his gaze on the expanse of blue-green sea that stretched to a cloudless horizon. He took another sip of coffee, aware of Edward's speculative gaze.

The older man had been a mentor to him for twenty years, ever since Demos had loitered longingly by his yacht, eager, desperate for work. Jameson had employed him, and later helped him win a scholarship to study marine architecture. He would have given him much more, but Demos had refused. He would pay his own way, earn his own money, provide for his own family. And so he had, for as long as he'd been allowed.

'As far as I know,' Edward remarked mildly, 'he is not the kind of man to be interested in yachts.'

Demos smiled. 'No?'

Edward waited, too shrewd and too polite to ask Demos directly why he was fishing for information about Paranoussis.

'And his family?' Demos asked after a moment. 'What do you know about them?'

Edward's mouth tightened imperceptibly. 'His wife died ten years ago, or round about that. He has one daughter. I met her once or twice, back when she was a child. Pretty girl, quiet and well-behaved. Although from what I've heard she's now a bit of a liability.'

'How so?'

Edward shrugged. 'Wild, reckless, always getting herself in the tabloids.'

Demos nodded thoughtfully. In some ways he was surprised he hadn't seen or heard of Althea before last night. He undoubtedly frequented Athens's nightspots, although in general he preferred more discreet venues. He didn't read the tabloids, however, and he realised with a wry grimace that he was probably considered too old for Althea's crowd.

'How old would the daughter be now?'

'Twenty-two? Twenty-three?' Edward leaned forward, his curiosity piqued. 'Why do you ask, Demos? What is your interest in her?'

'I met her last night.'

'Met?'

Demos chuckled. 'Yes, met. That's all. And I wondered.' Yet it was more than that, Demos knew. A lot more. He was not about to tell Edward the truth. That he'd met her and wanted her. That she intrigued him, challenged him, fascinated him in a way no other woman had.

And he wasn't even sure why.

Edward returned to his breakfast. 'I would usually warn you off colleagues' daughters,' he said wearily, 'knowing your reputation with women. But this time I won't bother. I'm not sure a girl like Althea Paranoussis has a heart to break—or at any rate a reputation that needs guarding.'

It was a more polite way of saying what Angelos had said last night, and Demos was surprised by his instinct to defend Althea from her accusers. What little he knew of her supported such statements. He thought of Angelos's easy familiarity with her, with her body, and suppressed a grimace of distaste. Althea didn't need defending. Perhaps she didn't even deserve it.

And yet...

'Although,' Edward continued thoughtfully, 'I've heard from various business associates that Paranoussis wants to see his daughter married.'

'Married?' Demos repeated, nearly spluttering over his coffee. He thought of his conversation with her last night; she was determined to stay clear of marriage. A free spirit—just what he wanted.

Edward sipped his coffee. 'Marriage would steady her as well as the family's reputation.'

'Is it that bad?' Demos asked. Most rich young girls were spoiled and shallow, at least in his experience. Surely Althea's brand of entertainment was no worse than theirs?

'Perhaps not to you,' Edward replied with a little shrug, 'but Attica Finance is a conservative organisation. Spiros wants to see his daughter taken care of.'

'And out of the way?'

'Out of trouble, perhaps.' Edward paused, his fork suspended halfway to his mouth. 'Does it matter so much to you, Demos? She's just a girl.'

*Just a girl.* Edward's tone was casually dismissive, yet Demos was shrewd enough to see the flicker of suppressed interest in Edward's eyes.

He leaned back in his chair. 'I don't know how much it matters,' he finally said, choosing to be candid. 'I just met her.'

'She might suit you,' Edward replied. His eyes sparkled with both mischief and possibility. 'Like you, she wants to have a good time. Socially she has all the connections...'

'I don't need connections.'

Edward's little shrug was a silent eloquent reminder of his background, Demos knew. The son of a grocer, with his mother now married to a butcher and still living in a working class suburb of Piraeus. No matter how his life looked now, he'd always know where he'd come from.

'Think about it,' Edward said lightly, and began to butter his toast. 'Paranoussis would be willing to arrange something...see her taken care of, as I said. And a man like you—wealthy, industrious—would impress him suitably.'

Demos smiled. 'You want me to *marry* her?' His voice had a lilt of disbelief.

'Do you plan ever to marry?' Edward asked, and Demos considered the question.

'Perhaps. Eventually,' he said at last.

'The party circuit grows old, my friend,' Edward said, a weary world of experience in his voice, and Demos nodded in agreement.

He was already feeling it. But marriage…?

That was another proposition altogether—and not a very welcome one. Yet even as he dismissed it his mind turned over the possibility. He'd always supposed he would need to marry at some point. He pictured Althea in the role of his wife and found it surprisingly invigorating. She wouldn't be an innocent, irritating little miss; she'd be fiery and spirited…in bed as well as out of it. His lips curved in a smile of imaginative appreciation.

'I imagine Althea will be married off within the year,' Edward continued with a shrug. 'Or sooner, if she continues to push her father. He's had enough.'

Demos's gaze snapped back to Edward's. 'He can hardly force her—'

'Can't he?' Edward arched one eyebrow, ever shrewd. 'She could be cut off without a cent, or an opportunity to earn one.'

'She's educated—'

'Actually, she isn't. She was expelled from school at seventeen, for bad behaviour.'

Demos sat back, considering. Althea might not have an education, but she was surely intelligent. She would survive if her father actually did make good on his threat and cut her off.

Anyway, he dismissed with a little shrug, Paranoussis was most likely just threatening Althea in an attempt to curb her behaviour. It had nothing to do with him; all he wanted was to see her again.

And, he acknowledged, his lips curving wryly, a bit more than that…

He turned back to Edward, who was watching him with growing curiosity, and smiled blandly.

'How about some more coffee?' he asked, and Edward's own smile widened as he poured.

Althea had taken the bus from her father's house in Kifissia to an upscale boutique on Tsakalof Street in Kolonaki. Her father gave her very little pocket money, and she was careful with what she had.

Now she sat on a leather-cushioned bench as Iolanthe tried on pair after pair of high-heeled sandals. 'Everyone has these now,' she said, twisting her ankles to catch a better view of the sandals' gaudy beading. 'Don't you want some, Althea?'

Althea shrugged and eyed the pointed heels. 'They look like a deathtrap for the dance floor.'

'And you *are* a good dancer.' Iolanthe met Althea's eyes in the mirror and winked. 'I saw you and Angelos last night.'

Althea remembered Angelos's hands pulling on her hips, pulling her towards him, and suppressed a grimace. She stretched her arms along the railing behind her and shrugged. 'You and everyone else at the club.'

'He was telling everyone you ditched that man you left with to be with him. Is that true?'

*Damn him*, Althea thought, but she shrugged again. 'Ask me no questions and I'll tell you no lies.'

'Who *did* you leave with? He looked…' Iolanthe paused, her eyes flicking over her own appearance, the smooth, girlish curve of her cheek and shoulder, the sequined top and fringed skirt she wore. 'Old,' she finally said, and Althea laughed.

'Oh, he's old. At least thirty.'

'Older than us,' Iolanthe protested, and Althea shrugged again.

Compared to Iolanthe, nineteen years old and determined to have fun, *she* felt old. Sometimes she felt ancient.

'Anyway, you left him?'

'After a while,' Althea replied. 'Now, are you going to buy those sandals or not? I'm hungry, and there's a café right across the street.'

'So you did go back with Angelos!' Iolanthe kicked them off and a sales assistant came forward to replace them in the box.

'Would madam like the sandals…?'

'Yes, yes—ring it up.' Iolanthe waved a hand and turned back to Althea. 'Well?'

'What do you think I did?'

'Althea…!' Iolanthe pouted. 'You never tell me what you get up to. I have to hear it from some man—or, worse, the newspapers.'

'The tabloids will print anything,' Althea dismissed in a bored voice. 'Now, let's get a coffee.'

They sat outside, the sun hot despite the brisk breeze of early spring. A steady stream of shoppers moved by in a blur of colour and chatter, the trill of a dozen different mobile phones punctuating Iolanthe's insistent pestering for details.

Althea took a sip of coffee and realised how tired she was. Tired of pretence, tired of everything, and she'd been tired for so long.

She sighed, smiled, and returned her attention to Iolanthe's chatter. Her lifestyle had suited her for the last several years. It would continue to do so.

She didn't really have any choice.


'Hello, big brother.'

Demos closed the door of his loft apartment in Piraeus harbour and turned around slowly. Brianna sat sprawled on his sofa, grinning up at him as she lazily swung her feet.

Demos watched her, and a chill of apprehension crawled through him. He shook it off with determined force and moved to greet her. 'Hello, Brianna. This is…a surprise.' He didn't think she'd ever been to his apartment before, and he wondered how she'd got in.

'I got the key from the woman downstairs,' Brianna said, in answer to his silent question. She smiled impishly. 'She thought I was one of your women, but when I explained I was your *sister*…'

'Of course.' He forced himself to smile as he kissed her cheek, his gaze sweeping over her outfit—what there was of it. 'Your skirt is too short.'

Brianna pouted, and Demos tried to smile again. His sister was looking at him with too much hope and fear in those wide, wistful eyes. Turning away, he went into the kitchen. Brianna scrambled up from the sofa to follow him.

'You're one to talk,' she said, hands on her hips, and a smile tugged at Demos's mouth despite his intention to remain stern and aloof with his littlest sister. He could never stay so for long; he'd given her bottles as a baby, had taught her to walk, had *promised*...

No. He wouldn't think about that. He turned back to her, arching one eyebrow as he smiled playfully. 'Am I? I don't wear skirts.'

She giggled, a practised girlish trill that grated on his nerves, his memories. 'Demos! I meant that the women you're seen with do.'

An image of Althea in that scrap of a silver dress flashed through his mind. The defiant sparkle of those sea-coloured eyes, the sensual promise of her smile. He wondered yet again why she intrigued him so much. Why he couldn't stop thinking about her. 'What do you know about the women I'm seen with?' he asked, and Brianna shrugged.

'I see the papers.'

'Mama lets you read those?'

'Demos, I'm twenty-one! She can't stop me!'

Demos frowned, once more taking in his sister's painted face and tarty clothes. She was trying to look sophisticated, he supposed, and missing by a mile. 'When are you going to settle down and marry a nice boy? Someone from the neighbourhood? That Antonios, the chemist's son—he's always been sweet on you.'

Brianna made a sound of disgust, her eyes sparking. 'Antonios! He's an oaf.'

'A nice oaf,' Demos countered mildly, although he observed her clenched fists and sparkling eyes with another chill. 'He has a steady job—'

'I want more than that!' Brianna stood with her hands on her hips, her chin and chest thrust out aggressively. She looked so defiant, so determined, that Demos paused, the chill intensifying once more to a deep remembered dread. He recognised the glitter in Brianna's eyes, the trembling of her lips.

For the last eight years he'd kept his distance—for her sake as well as his own. Because he'd believed it was the right thing to do. Brianna needed him too much, looked up to him too much. She always had—ever since he'd held her as a baby in his arms and she'd reached up and lovingly grabbed his chin. Sometimes it felt as if she'd never let go. She'd wanted him to be father, friend, saviour.

And he never could be.

Now, observing her desperate, defiant stance, Demos realised how those eight years had lulled him into a sense of security. Peace. Both began to crumble.

'Brianna,' he asked gently, 'why are you here?'

He saw a flicker of uncertainty chase across her features and his dread deepened, pooled icily in his stomach. His only contact with Brianna had been his intermittent visits to where she lived with his mother and stepfather, Stavros. Only twenty minutes away, yet it was another part of the city entirely—another world. Working class, respectable, conservative. So unlike this spacious, airy apartment, positioned above Piraeus's nightclubs and shipping offices, both businesses vying for space and trade in Athens's ancient and busiest port.

Yet now she was here, visiting him. Needing him. Looking at him as if he could fix all her problems when he couldn't.

He knew he couldn't.

'I wanted to see you. I never see you any more...' she began, with a toss of her head, but he heard the tremble of need in her voice and something inside him crumbled and broke. Again.

He turned and took her by the shoulders. Her cheeks were still as round and soft as a child's. She was, he reflected, despite the make-up and clothes, nothing more than the frightened little girl he'd comforted during storms, played endless games of cards with on rainy afternoons. The little girl who had gazed trustingly up into his face and asked, *'You'll never leave me, will you?'*

And, damn it, he had said he wouldn't.

'Brianna,' he asked gently, 'what's wrong?'

'I want to come and live with you!' she said in a rush. Tears brightened her eyes and she blinked them back. 'Mama and Stavros are tired of me. They want me to marry, like you said. But, Demos…! I don't want to.' Her eyes widened, and a tear splashed onto his thumb.

He gazed down at her for a moment, at the need and fear so open and endless in her childish face, before he released her and moved out of the kitchen, back into the main space of the apartment. Through the sliding glass doors that led out onto the wide balcony he could see the aquamarine glint of Piraeus's main harbour. He had been out on that water less than an hour ago, his eyes and mind on an endless horizon. Now, with a resolute sigh, he turned back to face his sister. 'Why don't you want to marry?'

'Why don't *you*?' she tossed back, and he shook his head.

It was a question his mother asked him every time he went to her house. She'd ply him with her spinach pies and meltingly sweet *baklava* and then demand to know when he was bringing home his bride.

Demos just ignored her; there was no point in explaining that he didn't want a wife, a family. He'd had the responsibility of one since he was twelve. He didn't need any more.

He didn't need *this*.

'Marriage would be good for you,' Demos said, his voice turning brusque.

Brianna let out a choked cry. 'You hypocrite! You're allowed to live alone, go to wild parties, have affairs and lovers—'

'Brianna…' Demos warned in a low voice. But she was too furious to take heed, or perhaps even to hear.

'You get to do everything you want, to enjoy life,' she cried, 'and yet you want me to settle down like Mama did, like Rosalia and Agathe did, whether I'd be happy or not! You don't care about any of us now that you're rich, do you?' She stood there trembling, her fists clenched at her sides, tears streaking down her cheeks.

'I care about all of you,' Demos retorted. 'I always have.' He felt a tide of fury rise up in him, threatening to drown him in memories and regrets, and he forced it back down. 'More than you could ever know, Brianna.'

'Some way you have of showing it! You haven't been to see Mama in weeks. We still live in a house half the size of this apartment—'

'Brianna—silence! You are talking about things you know nothing about.' Demos slashed a hand through the air. 'Nothing,' he repeated in a steely voice.

Brianna shut her mouth and stared at him with wide frightened eyes. Demos regarded her for a moment, so angry and afraid, so *young*, and then with a muffled curse sank onto the sofa and raked a hand through his hair.

'What do you mean, Mama and Stavros want you to marry? They can't force you, surely?'

'No…' Brianna admitted in a small voice. 'But they're always hinting at it.'

'Hints don't mean anything. Mama's been hinting to me for years.' Admittedly her hints had the force of a sledgehammer, Demos thought, managing a wry smile. He was gratified to see Brianna give a tremulous little smile back.

'Yes, but they won't let me go out! I'm only twenty-one, Demos. I want to have fun…like you do.'

Demos jerked his head up and met Brianna's pleading

gaze. *Like you do.* The three words had the force of an accusation. A judgement. Even though Brianna did not intend them to be.

He didn't want Brianna to have fun. Not like he did. Never like he did.

He *was* a hypocrite.

He wanted her to be safe, cared for. Protected. He just couldn't be the one to do it. Not for Brianna's sake. Not for his.

'Like I do?' he repeated slowly. He'd never considered himself to be wild. He was careful in his entertainment, choosy with his partners, but still he revelled in his freedom, revelled with a determination borne of too many years of self-denial.

Freedom, he acknowledged now with tired truthfulness, that was paling the longer he experienced it. He wanted more out of life. More for Brianna, more for himself.

He had just never expected it to be marriage. Marriage… unending, stifling responsibility…someone always needing him, never satisfied, never enough.

Althea didn't need him at all. The thought made him smile.

'Demos…?' Brianna said in a halting voice, and his gaze snapped back to her as he nodded in grim acceptance.

'You can stay the night. I'll take you out to dinner.' He forced a smile. 'We'll have *fun*. But tomorrow I'm taking you back home, where you belong.'

'It's not fair—'

Demos held up one hand in warning. 'Don't,' he said in a hard voice, 'tell me what is and is not fair.' He softened his tone to add, 'It's best for you, Brianna. Trust me. I know this.'

That evening he took Brianna out to a reasonably trendy taverna—enough to impress, but hopefully not to entice. After she was in bed he called his mother.

'Demos!' Nerissa Leikos's voice sounded strained with anxiety over the telephone. 'I was so worried… Thank God she is safe with you.'

'Yes…but, Mother, she is unhappy. I am…' Demos chose his words carefully '…concerned.'

The silence on the other end of the line told him enough. There was cause for concern, for fear. 'Is she in danger?' he asked quietly. 'Does she need care?'

'She needs to be married,' Nerissa said flatly. 'She is the kind of girl who gets into trouble on her own, Demos. She sees you—'

'What about me?' Demos asked sharply.

Nerissa sighed. 'Demos, it is different for a man. You may do as you like, go out as you like. But Brianna—she is young and easily influenced. And you know her history, how easily she can become…distraught. If she were protected in a stable relationship… If she saw *you* in a stable relationship…' Nerissa trailed off delicately.

Demos knew what his mother was implying. Her hints had never been subtle. She wanted him married…for Brianna's sake as well as his own. And for the first time he considered it, the image of Althea and her teasing smile flashing through his mind with seductive promise.

Perhaps in one fell swoop he could influence Brianna— show her something more positive than the playboy antics she'd been watching from afar.

Perhaps his marriage would be good for Brianna, good for Althea. Good for him. Perhaps it was time.

He sighed. 'Thank you for telling me. I'll bring Brianna back tomorrow.'

'It will be good to see you here, Demos.'

Demos shrugged off the guilt that threatened to settle on him like a shroud. He couldn't remember the last time he'd been at his mother's house. There were reasons he didn't go back home. Home… His mother's house had never been his home. Nerissa had married Stavros when Demos was twenty-four, just when he'd started making money, trading the provision of a million-aire for that of a working-class butcher.

Demos's mouth twisted in sardonic acknowledgement of his own snobbery. Stavros provided decently for his wife and family, yet Demos could have given them so much more.

'Yes,' he said at last. 'It will.' But his words sounded hollow to his own ears, and as he severed the connection he was left staring into the darkness, lost in the shadows and memories of his past.

# CHAPTER THREE

'FOUND you.'

Althea looked up from the book she'd been engrossed in and her eyes widened in surprise, awareness prickling along her bare arms. Demos Atrikes sprawled in the chair across from her, grinning with the gloating satisfaction of a little boy. Although there was nothing boyish about the sensual glint in his eyes as his gaze roved over her.

Althea swallowed and looked away. She forced herself to idly turn a page of her book. 'Am I meant to be impressed?'

'Of course.' Demos's gaze flicked over her once more, lingering on the book in her lap. 'I didn't expect to find you in a library.'

'Oh? Where did you expect to find me?' Althea slipped the book into her bag and raised one haughty eyebrow, her lips curving with sardonic mockery. 'In a club? A boutique? A salon?'

Demos just smiled. 'You're different,' he said. 'I like that.'

'And I'm so thrilled to oblige you.' Althea reached for her bag as she began to stand up. Demos checked her with one hand.

'Don't be offended,' he said with a little smile. 'It was a compliment, you know. "Thank you" is usually the expected response.'

Althea shrugged his hand off and slipped her bag onto her shoulder. 'You really don't know anything about me.'

'I know your name. Althea. It means healing.'

'You've done your homework,' she acknowledged, her eyes flashing. 'Good boy.'

Demos grinned lazily. With irritation, Althea realised she was simply amusing him. He wasn't one of the callow, spoiled young men she was accustomed to, boys who were all too easily put off by her put-downs. Demos Atrikes had too much confidence, too much ease and comfort in who he was for her stinging little remarks to be anything more than a diversion.

'Have dinner with me,' he said, and although he spoke it like an invitation, Althea heard the command in his voice. Demos Atrikes was a man determined to get what he wanted. 'Please,' he added mildly, his eyes glinting with amused appreciation, and Althea let out an exasperated sigh.

'Since you put it so nicely,' she said, and he chuckled.

'I'll pick you up tonight.'

'Maybe I have plans.'

'Maybe you don't,' he replied, unfazed, his gaze holding hers, and Althea shrugged, suddenly weary of being defiant. She didn't have plans, and she was honest enough to admit she wanted to see Demos again.

What was it about him? she wondered. Was it his age, his experience, his confidence? Or was it something deeper and indefinable that lurked in those silvery eyes, in the set of his jaw? Something that revealed itself in tiny but telling ways? When he dropped his blazer over her shoulders? When he said please?

When he asked her about herself, and waited as if he really wanted to know the answer?

Or were these simply deceits designed for one purpose? To get what he wanted. Her.

Even as her mind buzzed with unanswered questions she hesitated, torn between her own desire and the need for self-protection. Distance. She pursed her lips, prepared to form a quelling rejection.

Demo waited, all too confident, and she found herself sighing. Smiling, even. 'All right. Pick me up at seven. If you've done your homework, you know where I live.'

Demos still sat sprawled in his chair, his long legs stretched out with careless elegance, his eyes flicking over her with sleepy yet considering thoroughness. 'Of course I do.'

'Good.' With that, Althea turned and left. She didn't look back.

Later that evening she gave her reflection one final glance before turning away from the mirror. She hadn't known how to dress for her dinner with Demos, caught suddenly between who she appeared to be and who she wanted to be. Who she was…and who Demos thought she was.

Who she wanted him to think she was.

She sighed, impatient, uncertain. There were too many choices, and yet she acknowledged there weren't enough. She'd been playing the game too long to try to be real now. To want it. Demos might seem different, but he'd already made clear what he wanted. How little he wanted.

Her body. An affair. Cheap, easy, quick.

She still didn't know why she'd agreed to this date—why even now she was wanting to go.

She was bored, but she'd been bored for so long it hardly mattered. She wanted something different, something more, but Demos hardly seemed to offer it.

Unless she really did have some naive, ridiculous hope that even now someone could see her for who she really was. Save her.

Althea laughed aloud, a hard, unforgiving sound in the solitude of her bedroom. That wasn't going to happen. She didn't even want it to. She couldn't.

A car pulled to the kerb in front of the townhouse, and Althea saw Demos climb out from the driver's side. It was a sports car, dark in colour and discreetly expensive: the car of a man who had money to spend and yet chose not to flaunt it.

She moved away from the window, her heart-rate accelerating, just as the doorbell rang.

Althea waited while Melina answered it. She listened from the upstairs hallway while her father and Demos exchanged stiff, civil greetings. When the conversation dwindled into awkward silence, she made her entrance.

She heard Demos draw his breath in sharply as she came down the stairs, and she smiled. She liked it that he couldn't help but reveal his attraction to her, and she needed the surge of power it gave her.

She met Demos's eyes and saw them flare silver with awareness as his lips curved into a slow, knowing smile. Despite her resolve, she felt a surprising spark of answering attraction in her belly, felt it spiral upwards until she was breathless.

She sucked needed air into her lungs and forced herself to keep smiling.

'You look beautiful,' Demos said, one hand clasping her elbow firmly, drawing him to her. 'I've made a reservation at a fish taverna in Piraeus. You like seafood, I hope?'

She gave a shrug of assent and they said their goodbyes to Spiros, who watched them with a narrowed, speculative gaze. Outside, Demos helped her into the low-slung seat of his car.

They drove in silence through Athens's night traffic, the taxis and mopeds a blur of lights on the city's narrow streets. Above them, ancient and crumbling, the ruined Acropolis was illuminated by both spotlights and a sliver of moon. Soon they broke away from the congestion of the city centre, and Althea saw the twinkling lights of Piraeus's harbour in the distance.

'I hardly ever go to Piraeus,' she said, breaking a twenty-minute silence. She glanced at Demos; he looked lost in thought, the muscles in his jaw bunched and tense. She wondered what he was thinking. Feeling.

'I live there,' he said.

'I suppose it's close to the shipping offices,' she ventured, remembering that he was a yacht designer.

'I have space at Mikrolimano,' Demos confirmed with a nod. They entered Piraeus, and even in the darkness Althea was struck by the mix: squalid tenements pressed against trendy boutiques and tourist shops. Despite the proximity to the harbour, it was a strange place for a man like Demos to live.

What had she expected? A chic penthouse flat in downtown Athens? A villa in a sophisticated suburb?

He parked the car on a narrow, shabby side street and moved to open her door. Althea climbed out cautiously.

He led her into a small taverna, panelled in dark wood and flickering with candlelight. There were only a few scattered tables, more than half of them taken. The owner, Kristos, greeted them with a hearty smile, and Althea wondered if Demos was on a first-name basis with every tavern keeper in Athens.

Despite the shabbiness of the neighbourhood, it was readily apparent that this was an upscale restaurant. Kristos ushered them to a private table in a secluded corner, spreading a creamy linen napkin in Althea's lap. She glanced at the heavy embossed menu.

'How did you find this place?'

'I used to be a fisherman,' Demos said, and Althea's eyes widened in surprise. 'When I was a teenager. Kristos bought *tsipura* from me.'

She shook her head slowly. 'You surprise me.'

'And you surprise me,' Demos replied, opening his own menu. 'So much so that I want to know more about you.'

'Such as?'

Demos's eyes glinted in the candlelight. 'Why were you expelled from school?'

It was such an unexpected question that Althea's mouth dropped open for a tiny second before she snapped it shut once again. 'Where did you learn that little titbit of information?' she drawled, her eyes on the menu.

'You can't really think it's difficult to find information about you?' Demos asked.

He watched her carefully, made her nervous. Althea gazed at the menu, her vision blurring on the words. Anchovy. Bream. *Skathari. Tsipura.*

'Not if you go digging,' she finally said, keeping her voice bland. Still, her eyes flashed as she looked up and Demos smiled.

'So what happened?'

Althea flicked her hair over her shoulders. 'I was naughty with the gardener's boy.'

He raised his eyebrows. 'How naughty?'

She gave a hard smile even as her stomach roiled with remembrance. 'Naughty enough.'

Demos leaned back in his chair. 'With a family like yours, I can't imagine that would be enough to get you expelled...even if the two of you were *in flagrante*.'

Althea reached for a bread roll and began to butter it with an air of unconcern. 'Probably not,' she agreed, 'if my father had wanted to make a fuss. But he didn't. He wanted to teach me a lesson, so he had me sent home.'

She broke off a piece of bread and popped it in her mouth. Why did she feel she'd said too much? There was too much knowledge in Demos's eyes, too many assumptions lingering there.

'I see,' he said, and reached for a roll himself. 'And did you learn your lesson?'

She hesitated before replying, 'What do you think?' Demos just smiled and said nothing.

They ate in silence for a few moments, until the waiter came to take their orders. Demos ordered the bream, and after a second's hesitation Althea ordered the *tsipura*.

'It's always fresh,' he said lightly, handing the waiter their menus.

Althea smiled. Or at least she tried to. Why was she so nervous? So jumpy? Somehow Demos Atrikes had slipped under her defences, under her skin. She felt exposed, raw. Real.

She didn't like it.

The waiter returned with wine, and after Demos had tasted it he poured for both of them.

'So,' Demos said, after they'd both sipped their wine, 'your father sent you home. And you've been in Athens since then?'

'No.' Althea set her wine glass down. Demos waited, and she found herself continuing. 'I stayed long enough to realise I was bored.'

'How long did that take?' Demos asked, one eyebrow arched.

Althea heard the judgmental note in his voice and wondered why it hurt. He was simply believing she was what she said she was. What she really was. She lifted her chin. 'A few months. Then I joined the crew of a marine research ship—out of Piraeus, actually. I did the cooking and cleaning for the research team.'

'Really?' The surprise in Demos's voice was blatant, and Althea could hardly blame him. She rarely spoke about her time on the ship. Most of her friends didn't even know she'd been, undoubtedly assuming she'd been sent to another school to wait out her majority, if they bothered thinking about it at all. 'Did you enjoy it?' he asked after a moment.

Althea traced one fingertip around the delicate rim of her wine glass. It was a simple question, really; surely he expected a simple answer? So she would give one. 'Yes.' She looked up, shrugging. 'But I didn't want to scrub floors for the rest of my life, even in the middle of the Mediterranean, so after two years I quit and came back home.'

'Did you ever think of returning to school?'

Althea's smile was hard and she lifted her chin. She wasn't about to trust Demos with the truth. 'No. Why bother?'

'Why, indeed?' He smiled faintly, damning her with his barely disguised condescension.

Althea's fingers clenched in her lap, balled her napkin into one frustrated fist. There was no point telling anything to this man, she reminded herself fiercely. Even if he surprised and discomfited her at turns, he was the same. He was the same as every other man who'd looked at her with that knowing glint, that speculative smirk. He was even honest about it.

So why was she still persisting in the impossible, *stupid* hope that he was different? Why did she want Demos Atrikes to be different?

Or did she just want *someone* to be different? she wondered bleakly. Someone, anyone…

'And so for the last four years,' Demos surmised, 'you've

been living at home, dancing and drinking and hosting Daddy's dinner parties.' There was no condemnation in his voice, only a faint, lazy amusement. As if that was what he wanted her to have done, who he wanted her to be.

And it was. Of course it was.

'More or less,' she agreed carelessly, and took a defiant gulp of wine.

Demos leaned forward. His eyes glittered and his voice was low. 'You know what I think, Elpis?'

'Don't call me—'

'I think you're bored. I think you're just about as bored as I am.'

'Bored?' she repeated, lifting her eyebrows in mocking incredulity. 'I can tell you this: I'm bored right now.'

He chuckled and leaned back, his long fingers raking through his hair, sweeping it from his forehead before it flopped boyishly back. 'No, you're not,' he said, with a tone of such certainty that Althea had to keep herself from cringing.

It was true, though. She wasn't bored. She was intrigued, intimidated, frustrated. And she had a feeling Demos knew she felt all three.

The waiter came with their meals, and Demos deftly turned the conversation to trivial matters as they ate their delicate, flaky fish. Every morsel was delicious, and with the good food and wine, the easy conversation, Althea found herself relaxing, her guard slipping if only for a moment.

'Why don't we take a stroll along the harbour?' Demos asked after he'd paid the bill, and Althea nodded her agreement.

Outside he led her down a narrow street which opened suddenly onto Zea Limani, Piraeus's harbour for the island ferries and hydrofoils. The pavement fell away to an endless black sheet of water, dancing with the reflection of fairy lights spangled on half a dozen ferry boats.

Demos led her along the quay. Below them, on a rocky beach, a couple of wild dogs scrapped among the washed-up detritus and fish, their excited barks heard over the steady slapping of the sea.

The air was salty and surprisingly fresh, and the voices of the ferry sailors carried across the water.

'Mykonos! Mykonos at eleven o'clock!'

'Amorgos! Ten o'clock! Leaving now!'

They were raucous siren calls, Althea thought, to places she'd never been but which sounded exotic, exciting. They reminded her of that first freedom she'd felt on the research ship: the endless expanse of water, the wonderful possibility of being someone new, of being herself.

She hadn't been on a ship since.

She leaned against the metal railing of the retaining wall and gazed out at the dancing lights. 'Do you like being on the water? In a boat, I mean?'

Demos joined her by the railing. 'Yes,' he said simply.

'So did I,' she said after a moment.

'You could do it again,' Demos said. 'Couldn't you?'

She'd thought of it; of course she had. But she knew she wouldn't. Couldn't. 'I told you, I don't fancy cooking and cleaning for the rest of my life,' she said lightly. 'There must be something better out there.'

'There is.' Her eyes were drawn to him, to the low, determined thrum of his voice, the dark intensity in his eyes.

'You, I suppose?' she said, meaning it to be a joke, a put-down, but Demos only smiled.

'Yes. Me. I want you, Althea.' His eyes were steady on hers, his voice calm and yet filled with an unshakeable certainty. 'More, perhaps, than you even know.'

'I suppose I should be flattered.'

'Aren't you?'

She shook her head, her hair tangling in the wind. 'Plenty of men *want* me, Demos.' She didn't bother to keep the scorn from her voice.

He smiled faintly, his eyes never leaving hers, never leaving her alone. 'For a night, perhaps. I want you for more than that.'

'How do you know?' she scoffed. She pushed her hair from her face with impatient hands, wishing she could end this conversation. Wishing her heart would stop thudding with awful hope.

*Hope.*

'I know,' Demos said. He hadn't moved, yet she felt as if he had. He was too close.

*Too close.* She never let anyone get this close, say these things, make her feel this way...

Her face flushed, and her heart kept on with its relentless drumming. She wrapped her arms around herself; the wind off the sea was cold.

'Then what? You want me for two nights? Three nights? I'm not a whore.' It hurt to say it.

'I'm not talking about a business transaction.' A hard note crept into Demos's voice, piercing her.

'Then a cheap affair? What a tempting offer.'

'One I haven't made,' Demos replied coolly. 'And what if I said I wanted you for more than that?'

'What?' She turned quickly, surprise flaring in her eyes.

He smiled, a slow curling of his mouth that she couldn't tear her gaze from. His hand tangled in her hair and drew her towards him. She didn't resist. 'I want you,' he said again, and then he kissed her.

She'd been prepared, or at least she'd thought she had. She'd known what he was going to do, what he intended, the moment he'd first spoken. Her eyes closed, her head fell back, and her heart froze as his lips brushed hers and then broke away.

'Look at me.'

Her eyes fluttered open and she took a shaky breath. 'Wh...what?'

'I want you to look at me,' Demos said. His voice was rough with impatience and irritation. 'Don't turn off your mind,' he said, 'and leave me your body. You may do that for other men, men like Angelos, but you sure as hell won't do it for me.'

He was asking for her soul. Althea shook her head in instinctive denial. Demos's hands crept up to cradle her face with gentle yet determined purpose, and his lips brushed hers again and again, before settling firmly over her mouth, taking sure possession.

Althea tried to close her eyes, but he wouldn't let her. His thumbs flicked at her lids so she was staring up into his face, up into those hard, dark eyes that demanded she acknowledge him, acknowledge and understand what was happening between them.

This felt like so much more than a kiss.

Finally Althea summoned the strength to wrench herself away. 'You don't ask much, do you?' she demanded in a shaky whisper and Demos smiled.

'It was just a kiss.'

'No, it wasn't.'

His smiled deepened with triumph. 'I'm glad you realise what is between us. We have something unique, Althea.'

'You barely know me—'

'That doesn't matter.'

'Actually, it does.' Now that he wasn't touching her, tempting her, she could think. She took a step away, her back pressed against the railing. 'I might interest you, Demos, because I'm a bit different from the scatty starlets you normally take to your bed. But I'm telling you now I'm not interested in being your novelty.'

'Are you sure about that?' he murmured, reaching for her again, almost lazily.

'Yes—'

He'd moved forward, bracing his forearms on the railing at either side of her, his body hard and hot against hers, pressing, demanding. His lips were a breath away from her own. 'My apartment is just a little way down the street…'

'Good. Then you can go home and I'll take a taxi back.'

He laughed, a sound of reluctant admiration. 'What? You're trying to prove something to me? I'd still respect you—'

'How touching.' Her back was pressed hard against the cold

railing. He touched her chin with his fingertips, tilted her head so she was forced to meet his enquiring gaze. She met his eyes with a fierce determination of her own. She would not weaken. She would not be cajoled or patronised.

'You don't need to play these games with me,' he said, and there was a distinct edge of impatience in his voice. 'Maybe it works with other men, Althea, but I told you. I don't play games.' His voice turned hard. 'I won't. I want you; you want me. It's simple.'

His unfailingly masculine logic made her laugh—a hard, biting sound. 'Simple, Demos?' she said, shrugging free of his almost-embrace. 'Or just easy?'

His eyes flared and hardened, his mouth thinning to a condemning line. 'Both, actually,' he replied coolly, and Althea flinched, felt the stinging disappointment of knowing that he was no different, and he certainly didn't think she was.

What a charade. What a farce. What a *lie*.

'Sorry to disappoint you, then,' she said quietly, her voice turning steely, 'but I won't fall into bed with you just because you bought me dinner. And that's just one way I'm so *different*.'

Demos smiled back, just as hard. 'Oh? Is this what you tell men like Angelos? Because it didn't look like that to me the other night.'

'You're not Angelos,' Althea snapped, and then took an instinctive step back against the railing as she saw a new feral light gleam in Demos's eyes.

'No, I'm not Angelos,' he agreed, in a voice of chilling civility. 'And the sooner you realise I can't be wound around your pretty little finger like him, the better off we'll be.'

He stepped close to her, heat and anger emanating from him in deep, powerful waves that had Althea pressing back even further.

'If I didn't know you better,' Demos murmured, 'I'd almost think you were afraid.'

'Angry, actually,' Althea forced out, and even managed to

meet that speculative silver gaze that knew too much and yet nothing at all.

Demos gazed at her for another endless moment, and Althea saw a new remoteness enter his eyes, his body. 'I'll take you home,' he said.

She heard the cool distance in his voice and knew she'd succeeded. She'd pushed him away, just as she'd meant to, so why did she feel disappointed? Hurt?

*Because you always do.*

She pushed that treacherous, terrible voice away and gave him a brittle smile. 'Good—you can save me the cab fare.'

The walked in silence down the quayside. Somewhere in the harbour a bell tolled, and with ragged cheers, the water slapping against its weathered sides, one of the ferry boats began to move out into the deep sea.

Demos led her down a side street to his parked car, opened the door and ushered her inside without saying a word. Althea leaned her head against the car's leather seat and closed her eyes.

They didn't speak as Demos drove out of Piraeus, leaving the harbour behind, and entered Athens's endless traffic. He navigated confidently down the city's main roads, and out again into the quieter suburbs, shaded by the Penteli Mountains. Althea sneaked a glance at his profile, saw the tension in his jaw, the hooded, thoughtful look in his eyes.

Demos stopped the car and Althea saw they were in front of her father's house. Her fingers curled around the door handle.

'This isn't the end,' Demos said quietly, although there was still an edge to his voice. She turned, and he gave her a hard smile. 'Do you think I give up so easily? I have more *hope* than that.'

Somehow she found a smile and pasted it on her face. 'What a challenge,' she murmured, and slipped out of the car, hurrying up the steps and inside before he'd even got out of the car.

The door closed with a soft, final click, and after a long moment she heard him drive away. She closed her eyes.

'So. Out again—and with God knows what—'

'Who, actually.' Althea opened her eyes. Her father stood framed in the drawing room doorway. His eyes were narrowed, his hands on his hips. 'It was a person, not a thing, Father.' She took a breath. 'Demos Atrikes, a yacht designer.'

'A playboy.'

She shrugged. 'Perhaps.'

Spiros shook his head, and Althea moved past him to the stairs. 'This can't continue, Althea. It won't.'

She stopped, one hand on the banister. 'I went out to dinner, Father, and I was home before midnight. You can hardly consider that outrageous behaviour.'

'No, but this is.' From the pocket of his dressing gown he took a folded newspaper and thrust it at her.

Althea accepted it with a little shrug of silent scepticism. The tabloids loved to report whatever tripe they could about her; she was used to it, although it could still have the power to hurt. She stared at the headlines for a moment, the words, the colours, the implications dawning on her slowly, sinking into her consciousness with ugly understanding.

*Daddy's Little Princess Parties Too Hard.* It was an exclusive, offered by one of her alleged lovers. She knew who it was—who had masterminded the whole thing. Angelos. This was his retribution for her rejection of him the other night.

She swallowed, gazing at the photograph of her in a club. It was the night she'd met Demos, she realised. Only three days ago, yet it felt like an age. She was dancing with Angelos, and he was reaching for her hips—

She thrust the paper back at her father. Someone had taken the photo on their mobile and sold it to the tabloids, she supposed. It hardly mattered.

'Well?' Spiros demanded, and Althea lifted one shoulder. 'So?'

'That's all you have to say? Your name, your face, plastered over the papers, shaming me, shaming yourself, *again*…' His voice trailed off suddenly, and Althea looked up in surprise. Ther were tears in his eyes. 'Althea, you cannot be happy like this.'

Her stomach clenched and she shook her head slowly 'When have you ever cared about my happiness?'

'What do you mean?' Spiros demanded, and his voice ros in frustrated confusion. 'When have I ever cared about anythin else? Do you think I *enjoy* seeing my daughter make a specta cle of herself? This isn't you, Althea—'

'Yes.' She cut him off, her voice cold, certain. 'It is.'

'Well, it won't be for much longer,' Spiros returned, and hi voice was just as cold as hers. 'I will not allow you to destroy yourself or the reputation of this family. I have watched i happen for the last four years, and I will watch no longer.'

Dread washed over her in an icy wave. Her father sounde far more serious and determined than he ever had before. Sh wondered distantly if she'd finally pushed him enough.

'What are you proposing, Father?' she drawled, her finger curling tightly around the banister. 'How can you stop me?'

Spiros's gaze was steely and certain as he stared her down 'This is going to end, Althea,' he said. 'For your own good a well as mine.'

The insistent trill of his mobile snapped Demos out of a reverie He was in his office, overlooking Mikrolimano. The sky and sea were both a hard, bright blue, and his mind should have been on the blueprints in front of him. Instead he'd been thinking of Althea. Again. Dreaming of the way she would feel, taste. He couldn't stop thinking about her, and it annoyed him. She was just another practised partygirl, he told himself— and then was forced to acknowledge that she was different. Deeper. Yet for some reason she didn't want anyone to know she was. He'd seen the book she'd slipped into her bag in the library: a dense biology text. Why on earth did she spend her carefree days reading that?

What was she hiding, and why?

Sighing, he snapped open his mobile. 'Yes?'

'Demos? It's Edward.'

Demos stretched back in his chair, his fingers massaging the back of his neck. 'What's going on?' he asked, for there was a note of concern in Edward's voice.

'I was just speaking to a colleague, and there's been a rumour about that young lady you were asking about.'

Demos sat up, his hand falling away. 'Althea?'

'Yes.'

'You sound rather grim, my friend. What is it?'

'Her father has arranged her marriage,' Edward said. 'As I expected he might. I only heard of it because the father of the groom in question is a colleague of mine.'

'Arranged her marriage?' Demos repeated. His eyes narrowed as he gazed out at the sea, the sun shimmering off its surface as if it were a metal plate. 'And does she have any opinion on the matter?'

'Actually, she doesn't know yet. But she will soon.'

'Somehow I think Althea will have something to say about this,' he said, leaning back once more. 'She doesn't strike me as the marrying type.'

'Perhaps not, but I do know that Spiros intends for the marriage to go through. He's threatening to cut her off without a euro if she refuses.'

'The man lives in the Middle Ages,' Demos said with a grimace of disgust.

'No, he lives in Greece. The Greece he knows, anyway. And that is perhaps a bit antiquated, but it's very real nonetheless. And so is this marriage.'

'Engagement,' Demos corrected flatly. 'Althea is not getting married.'

'You care so much?'

Demos ignored the friendly jibe. 'Who is the lucky man, then?'

'Angelos Fotopoulos.'

'What?' Demos's hand came down hard on the burnished

surface of his desk. His eyes flicked to the tabloid he'd scornfully scanned that morning. 'That piece of slime? I would have thought Paranoussis would at least choose someone respectable—'

'He comes from money,' Edward countered mildly. 'A good family.'

'He's a vulture!' Demos shook his head slowly. He remembered the flicker of disgust in Althea's eyes when she'd seen Fotopoulos, and knew that no matter what sexual history they had between them she wouldn't marry him.

He wouldn't let her.

'Demos?'

'Thank you for letting me know.' His voice clipped, Demos severed the connection.

He sat at his desk, lost in thought, as the sun sank slowly to the horizon, sending long golden rays across the placid waters of the harbour.

Four yachts of his own design bobbed gently in the wake of a motorboat—the outward symbols of his success and status. Yet at that moment it felt like very little, and he didn't even know why.

He was tired of the party scene, tired of its empty entertainments. Yet he'd never wanted to shackle himself to a woman, a family, a *life*. He didn't want the crippling responsibility, the endless demands, the useless regrets.

He was done with all that. He'd been done with it eight years ago, when Stavros Leikos had plodded into his mother's life and assumed the mantle of responsibility Demos had worn since he was twelve years old.

And Demos had given it to him gladly. He had. He *had*.

He'd had no choice.

Yet now he had a choice: he had a choice to continue living his life with the careless and hardened indifference of a man who had seen and had it all and found it wanting. Or he could turn back to his responsibilities, his regrets, and face them once more.

The sky darkened to violet and the sun slipped beneath the

horizon, gone in an instant, leaving nothing but a few vivid pink streaks across the sky. And then those too were gone, leaving nothing but a stretch of indigo, and then nothing but darkness.

# CHAPTER FOUR

THERE were voices coming from the drawing room. Althea paused in the act of shrugging off her jacket. She could hear her father's strident voice, and then an answering murmur that was both confident and mild in its tone.

Her heart lurched and her body tensed. It was only two days since her conversation with her father, since his veiled threat that her behaviour would have to end. Nothing had happened, and now Althea wondered if something would.

Quietly she walked to the drawing room door and pushed it open with her fingertips. Spiros stood in the middle of the room, speaking to a man silhouetted by the sunlight streaming in from the long, narrow windows. He was tall, imposing. He had his back to her, and yet Althea knew with a deep sense of foreboding who it was.

'Althea,' Spiros said, and he was clearly trying to sound pleased. 'I believe you know our guest, Demos Atrikes?'

Demos stepped forward, smiling faintly, although there was still a remoteness to his expression that reminded her of their night on the quay.

'Yes, I do,' she said after a moment. 'I didn't know you had business with him, though.'

'I do—of a sort,' Spiros said. He looked as if he was bursting to tell her something, and Althea knew it was nothing she wanted to hear. She moved into the room with careful casualness and sat on a settee, curling her feet under her.

'Well, don't let me keep you,' she drawled, her eyes flashing briefly to Demos again.

'Actually, Althea,' Spiros said, 'the business we have—'

'Spiros, this is not—' Demos interjected, his face and words taut, but her father ploughed on relentlessly.

'—is you.'

Demo's mouth thinned and Althea sat up. 'What are you talking about?'

'Demos has come here to offer for your hand—'

'What?' Her eyes flew to Demos's face; it was still dangerously blank.

'—in marriage,' Spiros finished. 'And you would be wise to accept.'

Althea stilled. The words seemed to echo remorselessly in the room, in her mind. *Marriage*. Blink, she told herself. *Think*. Her mind sputtered to life, realisations, implications pouring through her, turning her weak. Then she drew in a breath, let the oxygen fill her, buoy her.

'Oh, would I?' she finally asked, uncurling her legs to stand, tossing her hair back over her shoulders. 'Fortunately, then, Father, I've never been wise.' She thought she heard Demos choke back a laugh, and annoyance spurted. She would not be his amusement.

'Althea, I told you what would happen if you didn't settle down,' Spiros said, and he sounded weary.

'You said you would treat me like a child,' Althea cut him off. 'Do children marry?'

'Some decisions need to be made for you.'

'Not this one.'

'You will marry,' Spiros informed her, anger turning him cold and implacable. 'Or I'll—'

'You'll *what*?' Rage streaked through her like lightning, hot and white and electric. 'What have you not already done?

Keep me on a leash? Restrict my freedom? Refuse to allow me to work—?'

'Enough!' Spiros bellowed. He trembled with anger, and Althea wondered if he would have a heart attack. At that moment she didn't care if he fell down dead at her feet. She was too angry, too appalled at the realisation that her father had betrayed her yet again.

*Marriage.* He was actually attempting to arrange her marriage, her *life*. And how? With what threats? She took a steadying breath, felt renewed strength flow through her veins. She would resist this. She had to. She couldn't marry a man, not any man—not even a man like Demos, who looked at her as if he understood, liked her.

No, he didn't. He just *wanted* her.

'You will marry because you are my daughter and I command you to,' Spiros stated. Althea opened her mouth but he kept talking, his voice steely and sure. 'And if you don't you will not be welcome in this house.'

She blinked, felt his words like a slap. 'Are you saying you'd throw me on the street?' she asked after a moment, her voice as cold as his.

Spiros looked taken aback at her frank choice of words, and Althea realised she shouldn't have pushed him.

'Yes.'

Where would she go? What would she do? Her mind raced with possibilities, scenarios. There was no one she could turn to. No one she could trust. No one who *knew* her…

'Fine. Shall I pack my bags?'

Surprise and unease flickered in Spiros's eyes. What had he expected to happen? Althea wondered. Had he thought she'd suddenly turn into the pliant little girl she'd once been? Did he still hope for that even now?

'Don't underestimate the limit of my power, Althea,' he told her quietly.

'How could I,' she flashed, 'when you're trying to play God?'

'Not God, but your father! And I *pray* to God every day that you will be a true daughter to me.' He raised one shaking fist. 'I will send you from this house with nothing but the clothes on your back—do you hear? If I have to. If that's what it takes—' His voice broke and he shook his head.

Althea stood still, silent, inwardly reeling.

'Spiros.' Demos's voice was quiet, yet it managed to still them both with its steely assurance. 'Let me talk to Althea. Alone.'

'I don't—' she began.

'Please,' Demos said pointedly, and Althea knew it wasn't a request; it was a command.

Spiros's mouth thinned into a hard line. 'As you wish,' he said. 'Perhaps you can make her see sense.'

He strode from the room, slamming the door behind him so hard that the windowpanes rattled.

It felt like the aftermath of a storm, Althea thought numbly. Or perhaps the eye of it. Demos stood across from her, relaxed, calm, and in control.

Control. This was about control.

She lifted her chin and tossed her hair back over her shoulders. 'You said this wasn't the end,' she murmured. 'And you were right. I'll grant you that. Was this what you had in mind when you said you wanted me for "more than that"?'

Demos smiled faintly, but he was still watching her with a speculative coolness that she didn't like. He didn't respond except to look at her, waiting. Waiting and watching.

'I'm not going to marry you,' she finally said. 'You do realise?'

'You may have no choice.'

'This isn't the Dark Ages.'

'I thought something similar, but it was pointed out to me that even so your father is a conservative man.'

'And what are *you*?' she flashed. She felt hurt and fear pierce her composure with icy needles, making her cold. So cold. 'Why are you here?' she demanded, now that she'd started to ask questions. 'Did you come here with a marriage proposal? Did you actually think—?'

'No.'

She stopped. Her arms had crept around herself, but she forced herself to drop them and stand tall and straight. 'No?'

'Not exactly,' Demos amended with a little shrug. 'I came here because I learned that you were engaged to another man.'

Althea's mouth dropped open. '*What?*'

'Don't you want to know who it is?' Demos asked, one eyebrow arched. 'Or rather, was?'

'It wasn't anyone because I was never engaged,' Althea snapped. 'If my father told you that, he was lying to you.'

'Was he?' Demos's gaze fastened on hers, unrelenting, his eyes as cold and hard as metal. 'Or was he lying to you?'

Her breath came out in a sudden rush as she silently acknowledged the terrible truth of his statement. Her father had told her that her behaviour would end, but she'd no idea he would resort to this. Marriage. Without even telling her.

'This is absurd,' Althea said, and Demos gave a little shrug of assent.

'Yes.'

It comforted her strangely—stupidly, perhaps—that he agreed. 'So my father arranged my marriage,' she said, and managed to keep her voice calm, unconcerned. She walked the length of the room in measured paces, coming to a stop by the windows that overlooked the street, cast in shadow by the fading sunlight. 'And then you came here and presented yourself as a candidate.'

'Yes.'

'Why?'

Demos was silent, and Althea looked over her shoulder at him. His eyes were as hard as ever, his mouth drawn tightly, his body set in lines of tense determination.

'You don't seem like the marrying kind,' she added. 'In fact, you told me as much yourself.'

'Circumstances change.'

'Such as?'

'I've decided I want to marry,' Demos replied flatly, and Althea knew he wouldn't be drawn. Not yet, anyway. Well, neither would she.

She turned back to the window. The sun had set now, disappearing behind the rows of townhouses. The Penteli Mountains were a ragged fringe on the horizon, leaving the street lost in twilit shadows. Her arms stole around her body once more.

'I don't understand,' she whispered, and knew Demos had heard her. He moved quietly to her side, laid one hand on her shoulder. Althea jerked under his touch, light yet firm, but he did not move his hand.

'You don't have to obey your father,' Demos said.

Althea turned around, took a breath. 'Of course I don't. And I won't.'

'He could make life very uncomfortable for you, though,' he observed. 'And somehow you don't strike me as someone used to discomfort.'

Althea lifted her chin even as she considered her father's threat. She had no money, no means. She didn't even have friends who would take her in. Iolanthe lived at home, and her parents would undoubtedly close their doors against a dishonoured daughter. How had this happened? she wondered. She'd been pushing her father, she knew, making him angry because she was angry, because she couldn't forget. She couldn't forgive.

She just hadn't thought it would come to this.

And yet she must have known that there had to be a breaking point. At some point one of them would snap. She'd just expected it to be her.

Except it wasn't her; she was still here, alive and whole. And though the future frightened her to her very marrow, at least it would provide an opportunity. A hope.

Hope. The word, the possibility, tormented her. The only hope she'd given Demos Atrikes was of a night in bed, and that was all anyone thought she was good for.

She turned away, still lost in her own spinning thoughts.

'Who was the other man?' she asked at last. 'The man he intended—arranged—for me?'

Demos paused, and Althea tensed in anticipation. 'Angelos Fotopoulos,' he finally said.

She whirled around. 'Angelos?' She shook her head. *'Angelos?'*

'Yes.'

'But he's…' She bit her lip. She didn't want to be honest with Demos. She couldn't afford even the tiniest window into her soul.

'He's what?' Demos asked. He raised his eyebrows in mocking query, although she saw a dark flicker in his eyes. 'A bore? A scumbag? A fashion disaster?'

A reluctant and unexpected bubble of laughter welled up inside her, escaped in a tiny breath of sound. 'All three.'

Demos gave her a hard smile. 'Of course if you prefer his sort—'

'I don't *prefer* anyone,' Althea snapped. 'I don't want to marry!'

Demos just shrugged, unmoved.

She lifted her chin. 'Why? Why do you want me so much?'

He looked nonplussed for a moment, and Althea wanted to laugh. She wanted to cry.

'Why?' Demos repeated. 'Why not?'

'That's not an answer.'

He shrugged. 'Because you're interesting, and beautiful, and—'

'Beautiful?' she interjected scornfully, and he raised his eyebrows.

'Surely you know that?'

Althea didn't answer. Yes, she knew it. She'd been told so since she was a child. What gorgeous hair! What lovely eyes! She'd hidden from her beauty at first, pretended it didn't exist. *She* didn't exist.

That hadn't worked, so she'd flaunted it instead. Exploited it. And, strangely, that was what had kept her safe.

So far.

'What's wrong with being beautiful?' Demos asked.

Althea forced herself to smile and toss her head. 'Nothing, of course.' She took a breath and stepped away from Demos. He was too close, too curious. 'So you've met me twice and you've decided you want to marry me. Why do I have trouble believing that?'

'*I* have trouble believing that,' Demos replied, 'because it's not true.'

Althea digested this statement for a moment, and then realised its implications. 'You just said you'd marry me out of *pity*,' she said slowly, 'so I wouldn't have to marry Angelos.' Her eyes flew to his face and she saw his look: stony, implacable. Silent. 'You're *rescuing* me,' she said in disbelief, and Demos's mouth tightened. Althea took a step back, shaking her head. 'I don't want to be rescued!'

'Good,' he said coolly, 'because I'm not interested in rescuing you.'

'Then why—?'

'I told you.' He cut her off. 'I have my reasons. You're interesting and beautiful and, frankly, I think you'd make a very good wife.'

'Well, I don't think you'd make a good husband!' Althea snapped, and Demos smiled. It was a slow, sexy curling of his mouth, and his eyes were smoky and grey and suddenly full of promise.

Althea swallowed.

'Actually,' Demos murmured, his voice as slow and sexy as that smile, 'I think I'd make a *very* good husband.'

Althea swallowed again; her mouth had turned very dry. 'How arrogant of you,' she managed crisply, and Demos's lips curved again with mocking knowledge.

'Is it? Perhaps.' He stepped towards her; she was pressed against the window, the curtains brushing her back. 'Why are you moving away from me?' he asked, taking another step. 'Are you afraid of me, Althea?'

He spoke with satisfaction at knowing her response to him, a satisfaction that made her furious, and yet even so the sound of her name on his lips was intimate. As intimate as their kiss. She'd never told him her name, and yet he knew it. He'd found it out. He spoke it now with a low, tender intimacy that he had no business feeling.

'I'm not afraid of you,' Althea said. 'I'm not afraid of anyone.'

'No?' Demos said softly. He took another step towards her so they were only a foot apart. 'You're very brave.'

'Don't patronise me.'

'Then tell me the truth.' Another step, and there was nowhere for her to go. Althea felt her heart bump against her ribs so fiercely it hurt. She hurt.

'We don't even know each other, Demos,' she said, trying to sound reasonable. To *feel* reasonable. 'We've met twice. It's hardly the basis for a marriage.'

'True, but since extenuating circumstances deem it necessary—'

'But they don't!'

Althea slipped away from the window, away from him. On the other side of the room she felt safe. She could breathe. Think.

'As you said, my father can't force me to marry.' She turned around to face him, smiling with grim humour. 'Oh, I know what he can do. He can cut off his money, he can throw me on the street, but he can't actually *force* me—'

'And is that what you want? To be completely cast out, cut off?'

'If there are no alternatives…'

'But there are.' Demos strode towards her once more. 'There's me.'

'You—' Althea choked in contempt, but Demos cut her off again.

'Yes—me. I'm a man who desires you. And whom I believe,' he continued in a soft voice that belied the dangerous intent of his words, 'you desire.' His eyes flashed and he waited, a handspan away from her.

Althea laughed aloud. 'Desire? That's your basis for marriage?'

'There have been many marriages based on far less.'

She shook her head. It wasn't enough. It wasn't *anything*. 'No.'

'Of course,' Demos continued, 'there are other considerations. A marriage between us would benefit me.'

'How?' Her eyebrows rose in challenge and her voice sharpened. 'Just how would this marriage benefit you? Because I really can't see it.'

'Can't you? I want a wife—a beautiful, well-connected, socially competent wife.'

'There are plenty of Greek girls who fit that rather pithy job description,' Althea replied coolly. 'You don't need me.'

Demos smiled. 'But you, alas, need me.'

She arched one eyebrow in disdain, despite the rage and fear that coursed through her in an unrelenting river of emotion. 'Do I?'

'And,' Demos continued, 'there are very few Greek girls who fit that job description and who have the other qualities I seek in a life partner.'

'Such as?' She'd meant to speak with the cutting derision that had sent young men scampering from her, clutching their wounded dignity as well as other parts, but there was a lilt of curiosity to her voice. She had betrayed herself, and Demos smiled.

'Someone who makes me laugh. Someone who intrigues me. And of course, as I said before, someone I desire.' His eyes flared and he held her gaze in silent challenge.

She shook her head, opened her mouth to frame a thought, a word, but none came. With a frustrated sigh she turned away. 'This is ridiculous.'

'We've agreed it's absurd,' Demos countered with a small shrug. 'But the facts remain the same. You need a husband. I need a wife. And while I've explained the benefits to me, I have not yet addressed the benefits to you.'

'That's because there *are* no benefits,' Althea snapped.

'Aren't there? I can think of quite a few.'

'You would,' she replied, hunching her shoulder, but Demos just smiled faintly.

'Of course there is my money. You're used to certain comforts, aren't you, Althea? I dare say you'd find life difficult without them.'

'Would I?' Althea turned to give him a hard smile of her own. 'Just another sign you don't know me, then, Demos.'

'And,' Demos continued, ignoring her, 'you seem like a woman who would enjoy the excitements of the world as well as the comforts.' He paused, his gaze flicking over her with aggravating thoroughness. 'Your life so far has bored you...'

Althea swallowed. How did he know? How did he see inside her head, her heart, so easily? The thought was terrifying. She licked her lips. 'You don't know—'

'You don't *want* me to know,' Demos replied. 'Do you? But I am a man who can offer you not just comfort or security, but something more. Opportunity.'

Opportunity. The word caught her, held her. 'What kind of opportunity could you offer me?' She heard the faint note of longing in her voice and wished she'd been able to disguise it. Wished Demos hadn't noticed it. But she saw by the glimmer of triumph in his eyes that he had.

Demos shrugged—an expansive, generous movement. 'Work? Study? Travel?' The words were like magic, firing her soul, her heart. 'Of course I would expect you to be with me for the majority of the time. But I'm not of an unliberated mind. I'm not,' he said with a new hardness in his voice, 'your father. I see no reason why you shouldn't pursue your own interests, finish school, take a job—whatever appeals to you.' Althea stared at him, a confusing array of emotions battling within her.

Surprise. Disbelief.

Hope.

'It appears,' he continued lightly, 'that you have not had such opportunities while residing with your father.'

She wasn't willing to give in that easily. She certainly didn't want to reveal that much. 'What are you talking about? My father has enough money to send me around the world twice—'

'He has enough.' Demos cut her off quietly. 'But does he do it? You never even finished school—'

'I was expelled!'

'Only because your father insisted you be sent home,' Demos countered. 'And refused to send you to another school.'

'I never said that.'

'I found it out.'

'You shouldn't have.' Althea drew a ragged breath. 'You shouldn't have,' she said again. She felt exposed. Raw.

Vulnerable.

She hated it.

'All I'm saying,' Demos said, spreading his hands out wide, 'is that you might have more freedoms and opportunities married to me than you do currently or would have if you were not to marry at all.' She opened her mouth to object, but he cut across her before she could frame a single syllable. 'Face the reality, Althea. This is Greece. A single woman…alone, penniless…you're not going to go far.'

'I have friends—'

He arched one eyebrow, his tone unsparing. 'Friends like Angelos?'

Althea gave a little instinctive shake of her head. Demos waited. The room was lost in shadow, dark and unknown. She moved to turn on a lamp, her mind whirling with possibilities both fantastic and frightening.

She straightened, saw the room had righted itself again, cast into warm pools of light. Comforting. Safe.

Except nothing felt safe.

She didn't like her life. Sometimes—often—she hated it. But it was safe. She at least had that.

Except now her father was threatening to take even that away from her, to leave her with nothing.

And here was Demos, offering her everything…for what in return? Certainly not for nothing. No, he wanted something. And not just a hostess or a well-connected woman. He wanted a wife…in his bed.

She faced him, tilted her head back so she could look at him from beneath her lids. 'A wife,' she said. 'In all senses of the word, I suppose?'

She saw surprise streak across Demos's features, and realised it was a question she shouldn't have asked. It was so glaringly, appallingly obvious. He'd already said as much.

'What would be the point otherwise?' Demos murmured. 'I intend to be faithful, and I'm not a monk.' He moved closer to her, closing the distance between them with easy, confident strides. 'And I would expect you to be the same.'

'Not a monk?' she mocked, and he touched her chin with one finger, tilted her face so her eyes met his own knowing, sardonic gaze.

'Faithful.' It was a word of warning.

Althea smiled and said nothing. Even now he actually thought she might marry him. And that if she married him she might have affairs. Both were so ludicrous, so impossible.

His finger left her chin to trace her jaw. She shivered under the tiny caress. 'Surely you want the same out of a marriage? There can be no question, Althea, that we desire each other.'

Desire. Yes, she'd felt desire. Terrible, helpless, *horrible* desire. Weakness, shame, pain.

'I never said we didn't,' she said lightly, and caught his hand with her own, intending to remove it from her cheek.

Mistake. His fingers closed over her own—gently, but with unmistakable certainty.

'Then why even ask?' Demos whispered. He brought her fingers to his mouth, touched the tips to his lips. 'Surely,' he continued, 'that would be one of the more pleasant aspects of our union?'

He smiled, and his teeth touched the sensitive pad of her fingertip. Althea yanked her hand away.

'Undoubtedly,' she replied, smiling although she felt sick. 'But if you want me in bed, Demos, you don't need to marry me.'

Something flashed across his face—what was it? Annoyance? Impatience? Or disgust?

'I thought,' he said after a moment, his voice turning cool, 'that marriage suited us both.'

'My father may back down.'

'Perhaps. Although it didn't seem likely when I spoke to him. You have pushed him too far.'

'You've seen the newspapers, I suppose?'

In answer he took a folded paper from his pocket and tossed it on the table.

'It's nothing really new,' she said after a moment. She raised her eyes to his and gave him a brittle smile. 'There's been worse.' She paused. 'I've done worse.'

'Undoubtedly,' Demos said again, and the word held only disdain. 'But since someone—Angelos, I presume, unless there have been others recently—has given his exclusive, there are a few more details than usual.'

She shrugged. 'I can weather it out.'

'It appears your father cannot.'

'You sympathise with him?' she asked. An accusation.

Demos paused, and she saw that dark flicker in his eyes again. 'No,' he said slowly. 'But I can understand why he wants to see you married.'

'Controlled.'

He shrugged. 'You may use whatever term you like.'

He folded his arms and the flicker in his eyes became a flash of fire. Anger. 'Or you can depend on the kindness of your friends. Suit yourself.'

Althea shook her head. Suit herself? She never had. She didn't even know how she could. She couldn't marry. Couldn't allow herself to be under someone's control, someone's body—

She suppressed a shudder. Demos wanted her—the temptress he'd seen in the club, the rebellious heiress, the good-time girl.

She couldn't be that girl. Not for ever. Not all the time.

She *couldn't.*

Althea took a breath and forced herself to shrug. 'I'm not the marrying kind, Demos,' she said, keeping her voice light. 'I told you that before. If you're looking for a good Greek girl—'

'I'm not.'

'What, then?' She arched one eyebrow in knowing mockery. 'A bad one?'

'You.'

She shook her head slowly, annoyed and yet defeated by his unshakeable arrogance. She was like a toy in a shop window, and he was the little boy pointing at it, saying, *That. I want that.* With no idea of the price. The cost.

To either of them.

'Love doesn't fit into this equation, does it?' she finally said, making her voice a bored drawl. 'You don't believe in it, I suppose?'

'Oh, I believe in it.' Demos laughed grimly. 'I have just had enough of it. I've got plenty of people who love me. I don't need another one.' His eyes met hers and they held a silent warning. 'I think we're both wise enough to the ways of the world not to go looking for love, sweetheart. Now, stop playing games with me. Because I told you I don't play them.' He stood before her, his body loose and relaxed, yet with a tense power radiating from him in forceful waves. 'You're not a shy virgin to blush at what I'm suggesting. You don't need to prevaricate, flirt—whatever other tricks you have up your skimpy sleeve.' He smiled. 'You want to marry me. You just don't want to admit it.'

His smile deepened, and she felt fury bubble up in her—a fury so consuming she shook with its force. 'Don't ever,' she said, her voice shaking too, 'tell me how I feel.'

Surprise flickered across his features, but he gave a little nod. 'Fine. Then you tell me.'

'Even I don't make decisions that quickly,' she said with a cool smile. 'I'm not giving you an answer now. I need time. Even my father will allow me a little time.'

'Don't be so sure.' Demos moved closer. He lifted his hands and rested them on her shoulders, drawing her firmly, inexorably closer.

Althea stilled, her mind sliding into numbness. Her eyes closed, her head fell back, and her body tensed, waiting, thrumming with a terrible expectation.

He brushed his lips across hers, little more than a whisper. She waited for the invasion, for the demanding knowledge of her mouth, her body. Her soul.

There was no demand. He stepped back, left her breathless with both relief and confused desire. Disappointment.

'You may have some time to think, but I'm taking you out tomorrow.'

'Why?' she asked mockingly, although her heart still thudded sickly and her mind swam just from that brief kiss. 'Aren't we already past the dating stage?'

Demos frowned. 'It might be a marriage of convenience, Althea, but it's still a marriage. We need to get to know each other.'

'You certainly don't know me,' Althea agreed with asperity, but Demos only smiled.

'I intend to find out.'

His smile lingered, and she felt his gaze sweep her with thorough, enjoyable assessment. She blushed under that gaze. Blushed and fumed.

And then he left. The door closed, leaving her alone, swamped in silence and uncertainty, her senses utterly overwhelmed.

The door opened again, and Althea saw her father framed in the doorway, his expression resolute.

'Well?'

'I'm not marrying anyone today, Father,' she said shortly. 'I thought you'd allow me at least a little time to decide the rest of my life.'

'One week,' Spiros declared. 'Otherwise you'll just get into more trouble.'

Althea shook her head. 'You believe the tabloids?'

'It doesn't matter what I believe, Althea! It's what the world sees and believes.'

'And what would happen?' she challenged. 'Your business would be ruined? Society would shun you? Do you honestly think I have that much power?' Her laughter rang out, hard and angry. 'I don't have *any* power, Father. You've made sure of that.' She shook her head. 'Tell me—with Angelos. Did you approach him, or did he make a deal with you?'

Spiros's glance slid away from hers. 'It was a mutual arrangement between families,' he said stiffly.

Althea laughed again. 'Mutual! Except I wasn't even part of it! Why Angelos? Don't you know what he's like? He's in those papers as much as I am.' She flung a hand to the discarded newspaper. 'He's the one in the photo!'

Spiros met her gaze once more, in an appeal for understanding that seemed utterly absurd in the situation. 'He's from a good family.'

'He's a pig.'

Spiros was silent, and for a moment he looked sad, his shoulders slumped in defeat, his hair in wild white wisps around his lined face. He looked old, Althea thought with a surprising pang of panic. Older than his sixty-four years.

'Do you think I do this for my business, Althea?' he asked, and there was deep weariness, a sorrow in his voice that surprised her. 'For myself?'

'It's hard to believe you do it for *me*,' she said with a bitter little laugh. 'Threatening to throw me out on the street? Trying to marry me to an animal like Angelos Fotopolous? How is that for my benefit, Father?'

Spiros shook his head. 'I thought you enjoyed his company,' he said. 'That the two of you together could be—'

'Never. I'll never marry him.'

'Then marry Demos,' Spiros urged. 'Perhaps I was wrong about Angelos. I'm not too proud to admit it. But you will marry, Althea. I won't back down on that, as cruel as it seems to you. You need stability, the security a man offers—'

'Security? A stranglehold, more like,' Althea scoffed. She shook her head, felt the creeping fingers of despair clutch at her heart. 'Are you really saying you'll cut me off with nothing if I don't marry?'

'Yes, I will,' Spiros said, and he sounded weary but resolute. 'Althea, I want you to be happy. I want you to be safe. And you are not. I know you are not.'

She stilled, his words trickling into her consciousness. 'But you've never cared about my safety, Father,' she whispered, and felt the betraying sting of tears. '*Never.*' She shook her head and set her shoulders. 'Don't justify yourself to me, Father. Not now. Not after all this time.'

She pushed past him towards the door, blinking back more tears, treacherous tears, tears she wouldn't let fall because she *never* cried.

She certainly wouldn't now.

Alone in his apartment, Demos sprawled on the sofa and knocked back his third shot of ouzo. Outside, a thousand pinpoints of lights glittered on the smooth black sheet of Piraeus's harbour, and in the distance he heard the faint, plaintive toll of a ship's bell.

He shook his head. What had he done? What in God's name had he done? Asking Althea Paranoussis to marry him? *Convincing* her to marry him?

He closed his eyes. He was a fool, controlled by a moment's desire and a lifetime of guilt.

He wanted her, yes. Still. Now more than ever.

Yet marriage? She'd said herself that she would have been satisfied by an affair. He'd been the one to push for more. To push *her.*

And why? To rescue Althea from her father's machinations? To rescue Brianna from the prison of her life, her mind?

Or to rescue himself? Relief from a way of life that had become empty and old, from the regrets and memories of the choices he'd made.

The choices he'd had to make.

Demos thrust his shot glass away and it clattered on the coffee table. He rose from the sofa to gaze unseeingly out of the window at a sea cloaked in night.

He'd freed himself from the shackling bonds of family, love, responsibility. He was *free*. So why was he offering to tangle himself yet again in that sticky web of need?

Althea's different, he told himself. She's like me; she doesn't want that kind of life. Marriage to her will be exciting, passionate. *Fun*.

Even as adrenalin shot through him at that thought he felt a lurch of dread. Guilt.

Marriage.

He turned from the window and his gaze fell on a framed photograph of Brianna—twelve years old, smiling tremulously. From nearly the day she was born she'd looked at him as a father, expecting him to fulfil her every wish, grant her every happiness. And he hadn't been able to.

And he'd walked away—walked away from her because it had seemed like the right thing to do.

Or had it just been the easy thing to do?

He'd failed her once before; would he fail her again now, when she needed him to provide a steadying, stable influence?

Could his marriage help Brianna? he wondered. Could it help Althea?

Could it help him?

At least Althea didn't need him—not like Brianna did. At least, Demos recognised hollowly, she was one person he couldn't fail. He swallowed, tearing his gaze from the photo, the memory, and then picked up his glass from the coffee table and went to pour himself another drink.

# CHAPTER FIVE

'WHERE are we going? Back to Piraeus?' Althea asked as the blurred lights of Athens's night-time traffic sped by in a stream of colour and the road opened up to the promise of water.

'You could say that.' Demos flexed his hands on the wheel, his jaw tight.

He'd been preoccupied and remote since he'd picked her up that evening, and Althea wondered if he regretted his proposal. Then she wondered if she wanted him to.

Would she be disappointed? Disappointed again, by a man finally, blessedly, leaving her alone?

She'd barely slept last night; she'd lain in bed and watched the moon slant silver beams on the floor, watched the shadows lengthen and retreat, and finally watched dawn break, faint and grey, as if afraid to flood the world with the healing light of day.

And while she'd watched her mind had run in hopeless circles. She'd imagined throwing her father's threats right back in his face, turning Demos down flat tonight, storming off alone into an unknown horizon.

She *wanted* to. She still might…if she had the strength, the courage to face life—the world—alone. The possibility was terrifying.

'I don't like surprises,' she said now.

Demos glanced at her, his eyes sweeping over her in careless judgement. 'Really? I would have thought you enjoyed a certain element of surprise.'

'Another sign that you don't really know me,' Althea replied coolly, but Demos just shrugged.

'Actually, I think the ability to be surprised is a good basis for marriage.'

'*Surprised?*' She didn't keep the note of disbelief from her voice.

'We'll never be bored,' Demos said with a shrug, and she felt a piercing stab of rage.

'I'm not going to marry you for your amusement and entertainment,' she told him. 'Hire a hooker or an exotic dancer if you don't want to be bored, Demos. Don't get *married*.'

Annoyance tightened his mouth, his eyes flashing dangerously. 'Don't twist my words, Althea.'

'I'm not,' Althea retorted. 'You don't want a good Greek girl, you said. Someone steady and staid who will give you babies on a yearly basis and bore you to death. Funny, because that's what most men want. Most men don't want to marry women like me. They want to *have* women like—'

'Althea—'

She heard the warning in his voice but chose not to heed it. 'No, you want to marry me because you want your own private entertainment,' she accused. 'A whore who isn't even paid.'

Demos was silent, but she felt the anger emanating from him in tense, powerful waves, felt it flood the small space of the car with terrible feeling.

She pressed her lips together and stared out of the window. How could she have thought for even a moment this might work? Last night she'd almost convinced herself that marriage to Demos might be a way out. An opportunity, as he'd said. As for what was required... She'd endured worse.

She could endure it again.

Yet now she was reminded of just what a prison marriage

was—covered in gilt, perhaps, but a prison nonetheless. And Demos would be her jailer.

He parked, and Althea saw they were at the harbourside—not the busy, commercial Zea Limani, but a smaller, more sophisticated harbour, bobbing with yachts and a few fishing boats. Mikrolimani.

The promenade was filled with cafés that spilled their patrons onto the pavement, and as Demos came round to open the door Althea heard the tinkling sound of china and laughter carried on the salty breeze.

She climbed out of the car, taking care not to touch him, but his hand closed firmly round her elbow anyway, and he steered her not to the street of restaurants and bars but to the sea.

'Where—?' She stopped, her heels skidding on the weathered wood of the dock, for she knew where they were going.

Demos turned around, impatience flitting across his features.

Althea folded her arms. 'Your yacht,' she said, and Demos arched one eyebrow.

'You mentioned you liked the water.' His voice was cool; she'd stretched his patience too far. 'Do you want to come on or not?' he asked, and although his voice was rough with impatience Althea heard something underneath, something almost strangely tender, and she realised he'd arranged this evening for her pleasure.

She had said she liked being on the water and so he'd brought her to his yacht. It was so simple. It really was.

At least it could be. Perhaps.

'I do like the water,' she said after a moment, and stepped aboard. Demos drew in the bow line that connected the yacht to its mooring and stepped in after her.

It was a beautiful boat, she saw immediately, lovingly furnished and cared for. She came into the main cabin and saw it was mostly made of burnished wood, glowing golden in the flickering lights from the harbourside.

There were two sofas, upholstered in dark leather, and by

the floor-to-ceiling windows, overlooking the harbour, she saw a table: cosy, intimate, and laid for two.

'Are we actually going to go somewhere?' she asked.

'It would be a rather poor choice of restaurant, otherwise,' Demos said, and she heard a ripple of amusement in his voice.

She looked up and managed a smile. 'Yes, I suppose it would.'

'What do you want? Dinner first, or the wide open sea?'

She swallowed, not wanting to admit even to herself how much it meant to her that he'd asked for her preference. It was such a small, simple thing—a courtesy most women expected. Demanded.

Yet it touched her deep inside, in a place she never acknowledged, a place that she pretended didn't exist.

'The sea.'

He led her to the cockpit and sat in the leather captain's chair, patting the seat beside him. She slid next to him as he started the motor, the boat thrumming to powerful life.

Althea watched as Demos steered the boat out of its docking. When they'd cleared the harbour he opened the throttle and the water stretched before them, a dark, endless sheet lit only by the yacht's runner lights.

Althea swallowed a giddy laugh as she felt the boat move beneath her, listened to its soothing steady hum and watched the sea speed by, churning white foam and deep, fathomless black.

Beside her Demos concentrated on steering, a faint smile relaxing his features, his movements controlled and graceful. He was, Althea thought, swallowing again, a beautiful man.

They sat in silence for a few moments, the only sound the purr of the motor and the churning of the waves, before Demos pulled back on the throttle.

'We're in deep water now,' he said. 'We can eat, if you like.'

Althea nodded, and slipped from her seat to follow him back to the main cabin. In their absence a Greek salad for two had been placed on the table, and wine had been poured.

'I have a cook,' Demos murmured in answer to her silent query. 'A right-hand man, really. He does everything.'

'You don't cook?' Althea quipped as Demos pulled her chair out for her and laid a napkin in her lap, his fingers barely brushing her thighs before he sat across from her.

'Actually, I do. I enjoy food, and I enjoy making it.' He smiled, his eyes dark, and raised his wine glass. 'To the future…whatever it holds.'

Althea nodded her agreement and took a sip. *Whatever it holds*… Yet there had been no questioning lilt in Demos's voice, no shadow of uncertainty flickering in his eyes. He knew what the future held; he was sure of it. He wanted something and he would get it.

She placed her wine glass on the table. 'This is very nice.'

'I'm pleased you think so.' Demos served her some of the salad, and Althea stared down at her plate. The salad was bursting with plump tomatoes, shiny black olives, and a sprinkling of feta cheese. It looked delicious, yet her stomach was roiling with nerves too much for her to attempt a mouthful.

'I don't understand why you want to marry me,' she said abruptly.

Demos's expression did not change. He took a bite of salad, chewing thoughtfully, before he answered. 'Which part don't you understand? That I want to marry at all, or that I want to marry you?'

Althea blinked. 'Both.'

Demos gave a little shrug and took a sip of wine. 'I told you yesterday. I need to marry.'

'*Need?*' Althea's eyebrows rose. 'Is someone threatening to toss you out on your ear? Or is that just me?'

He gave a faint smile, but Althea saw a hint of something like sorrow in his eyes as he steepled his fingers under his chin. 'No, but there are other pressures, Althea. Responsibilities.' He said the word so heavily—as if it were a burden he were laying down, or perhaps shouldering once more.

'What kind of responsibilities?'

He shrugged. 'A man in my position needs to think of the future. It's not prudent to be a freewheeling bachelor for all of my days.'

'It's not *prudent*,' Althea returned, 'to enter into a marriage with someone you barely know.'

He gave her the glimmer of a smile. 'True. But of all the women I've…known…you intrigue me the most.'

'But I've said you don't—'

'Yes, yes—you've mentioned before that I don't really know you. I don't think I need to know what your favourite bedtime story was to decide whether you would make a suitable wife. But, just out of curiosity, what was it?' He arched one eyebrow, his smile sardonic.

Althea pressed her lips together. 'I always liked the story of Theseus and the Minotaur,' she replied after a beat, 'but *Alice in Wonderland* was nice too.'

'They're rather different. I would have thought the Minotaur was a bit gruesome for a young girl.'

'I liked Ariadne,' Althea returned. 'She was the clever one, wasn't she? If she hadn't given Theseus the ball of string and told him what to do he would have been lost in the labyrinth along with everyone else.'

'True enough.'

'And,' Althea continued, stabbing a stray lettuce leaf with her fork, 'he repaid her by abandoning her on an island.'

'He got his comeuppance, though, don't you think?' Demos asked as he took a sip of wine. 'When he forgot to change the sails on his ship from black to white? His father was so distraught he threw himself off a cliff.'

Althea paused, then pursed her lips and shrugged. 'They both deserved what they got. If Theseus hadn't been in such a hurry to escape Ariadne he wouldn't have forgotten the sails. And if his father had just waited and *listened*—' She broke off, suddenly feeling exposed again, as if she'd been talking about something other than an old pointless story. As if she'd been talking about herself.

'He wouldn't have killed himself?' Demos finished, his gaze narrowing with speculation, and she shrugged.

'He wouldn't have ruined everything, at any rate.'

They were both silent, the only sound the gentle lapping of the waves against the side of the yacht. In the distance Althea heard the soft putter of another motor before it faded into silence.

'You still haven't answered me,' she said. A man, grey-haired and grizzled, came to clear the plates. Demos smiled his thanks and waited for his assistant to leave before he spoke.

'I thought I had. I've decided it's time to marry, and the woman I choose is you.'

She shook her head. 'It's not that simple.'

'Of course not. There are always other considerations, other people involved. Your father, for instance.'

'And for you? Who is forcing you to marry, Demos?'

'No one.' His voice came out hard, but then he smiled, awareness flaring once more to life in his eyes. 'I like it when you say my name.'

Althea sat back, dissatisfied. She knew Demos wasn't telling her everything, but she didn't even know the right questions to ask. Demos's assistant returned, this time with two plates of *souvlaki*, hot and fragrant with oregano and mint.

'*Efharisto*,' she murmured, and the man slotted her a quick smile before disappearing back into the galley. 'How did you go from fishing to yacht designing, anyway?' she asked Demos.

'I made my living on the harbour,' he replied. He spoke in an easy manner, but she saw something guarded in his eyes, and that flash of self-protection intrigued her. 'Carrying messages for captains and yachties, joining the crew of fishing boats—whatever I could find. An English businessman, Edward Jameson, hired me to crew on his yacht for a few weeks, and we became friends.' He smiled at the memory. 'He took me under his wing and eventually supported me through my course in marine architecture.'

'He sounds like a good man,' Althea said after a moment.

'He is.'

They ate in silence for a few moments, lulled by the shushing of the water, the gentle rocking of the boat.

Althea knew there were questions she should ask, things to consider. Important things. If she were seriously thinking of marrying this man she needed to know just what he expected from her beyond the basics. Where would they live? What would she do? Did he want children?

She swallowed a sudden incredulous laugh, for she didn't feel she knew Demos well enough to demand answers to such questions and yet she was thinking of *marrying* him.

Was she that weak, that pathetic, that she needed a man's protection even now? Even now, when her father had failed so spectacularly? When nearly every man she'd looked to for support and succour had proved to be a false friend?

Was Demos just another man in a succession of men who had disappointed her? Whom she'd allowed to affect her?

Or was he different?

'What are you thinking?' Demos asked as he poured them both the last of the wine.

They had finished their meals, and Althea propped her chin in her hand. 'What an insane proposition this really is.'

'It is, isn't it?' Demos agreed blandly, a glint of humour lighting his eyes, and suddenly Althea laughed—a hiccuppy kind of laugh, a sudden, startled sound that came from deep within her, from that place she'd forgotten about. Demos smiled, and she kept laughing; she couldn't stop. She covered her face with her hands, shaking silently, and she heard Demos's answering chuckle.

It felt good to laugh. She didn't often laugh—hadn't laughed like this, so it hurt, a healing pain, in a long time. Perhaps not since she was a child. She needed it, needed the release, the loosening of all her tightly held parts, her secrets.

Except those she knew she would keep to herself.

Demos reached across the table and grasped her hands with his own, although he didn't attempt to pull them from her face. 'Marry me, Althea.'

Another giggle erupted from her, and she shook her head. 'I've never laughed so much in my life,' she gasped out, and even though she still couldn't see him she knew he was smiling.

'I'd say that's one of the best reasons to marry me.'

She peeked out between her fingers. 'Laughter?'

'Absolutely.' Gently he prised her hands away from her face, his fingers skimming her cheek. 'We'll have a good time together.'

The words, so confidently spoken, made the laughter die on her lips as a new dread crept coldly through her. A good time. So little, so light.

'Is that all you want, Demos?' she asked. She turned to stare out of the window; the moon had risen and was bathing the sea in silver. 'A good time?'

He pulled his hands away and sat back in his chair. 'Yes, as a matter of fact it is.' There was an edge to his voice that made Althea realise she'd annoyed him—even disappointed him.

Demos exhaled impatiently and pushed away from the table, suddenly restless. Althea watched him out of the corner of her eye. His back was to her, his body stiff with tension.

'I think I've made my position clear,' he finally said, his voice cool. Cold. 'About what I want. It's up to you to decide, Althea, whether it's enough. Although your other choices don't look that attractive from here.'

'No, they don't,' Althea admitted quietly. She stared down at her empty plate.

The cabin was silent, the air heavy with expectant tension and unexplained thoughts. In the distance Althea heard the sound of another motor, before it too faded into the endless, yawning silence.

'Come with me,' Demos said finally, and, hesitating only for a second, Althea slid from her seat.

He led her back to the cockpit and sat in the captain's seat. Once again Althea sat next to him.

Demos took hold of the wheel, opened the throttle, and they began to speed through the night.

'Where are we going?' Althea asked after a second's silence.

Demos slanted her a quick questioning smile. 'Where do you want to go?'

'I don't…' Her words trailed away as she considered what Demos was asking her. She shook her head. 'I don't know,' she said quietly, and she felt as if she was admitting to a great deal more than the evening's destination.

The boat continued to glide through the water, churning up foam in its wake. On the horizon Althea saw a faint glimmer of lights, and realised they were already nearing an island—one of many that littered the Saronic Gulf, like a handful of pebbles scattered by a giant unseen hand.

'When you were on that research ship,' Demos asked, 'in the Mediterranean. Did you ever steer?'

'Steer?' Althea repeated incredulously. 'Of course not. I was the skivvy.'

A faint smile curved his lips and he stepped back from the helm. 'Now's your chance.' Althea stared at him in surprise but didn't move. 'You can take the boat wherever you want,' Demos said with a little shrug. 'Take it, Althea.'

And, after a second's hesitation, she did. She slipped into the cool leather of the captain's seat and curled her slick fingers around the wheel. 'I don't know what to do.'

'It's simple. Open the throttle if you want to go faster. Push it back if you want to slow down.'

'What if I hit a rock?' Her voice wavered.

'The sea's too deep.'

'Still…'

'I'm right here.'

Why was she so nervous? It occurred to her that she should have slid into the seat with a naughty little smile and opened the throttle as far as it would go. That was what people expected her to do; that was the kind of image she had cultivated for herself. *Cherished.*

Yet here, with Demos, she'd been herself, shown herself... and she hadn't even realised it. The thought made her feel both afraid and angry, and out of instinct she pushed hard on the throttle.

'Whoa!' Demos grabbed onto the back of her seat as the boat lurched forward, and Althea smiled grimly. 'You like to take it to the limit, don't you?' he murmured in her ear, and his breath made her shiver.

Still, he didn't command her to slow down, and after a moment Althea pulled back to a more reasonable speed. It was odd, being in control, her hands on the wheel, the horizon open before her.

Would marriage to Demos be like this?

She knew he wanted her to ask that question; he'd answered it by bringing her here tonight.

*Yes.*

She was tempted. She was terribly, treacherously tempted to believe that marriage to Demos could be wonderful, exciting. Different. An opportunity...a thousand opportunities.

Yet ultimately it was still marriage—still handing over her body and soul and perhaps even her heart to a man she barely knew.

A prison.

'I'm done,' she said, and pulled back on the throttle so the boat was idling in the water. 'Let's go on the deck.'

Demos nodded, and reached over to cut the engine. Then he led her out of the cockpit and onto the deck. The sky was spangled with stars, and a chilly breeze blew off the open water. Without the steady hum of the engine the night was silent and empty.

Althea stood by the railing, her arms wrapped around herself, and Demos stood next to her, his elbows braced on the railing. He waited, his expression fathomless, yet Althea felt his sense of expectancy.

He knew. He knew what she was going to say perhaps even before she did.

'You don't know me,' Althea finally said, after a moment. She'd said it before—an instinctive reaction, an accusation, even—but now she spoke quietly, with a certain sorrow that she knew Demos wouldn't understand.

'Tell me what I need to know, then,' Demos said.

Althea shook her head. 'It's not that simple.'

Demos looked up at her, his eyes glittering in the darkness. 'It can be.'

Althea shook her head. 'You'll get bored with me, Demos. I know men like you.'

'No, you don't,' he said with a firm coolness. Still she persisted.

'I'm a challenge. That's all you want.'

Demos eyed her for a long, tense moment. Somewhere in the darkness a foghorn bleated, a lonely, distant sound.

'We can have a good life together, Althea. We can have fun. Think of it.'

'*You* think of it,' Althea returned. 'Fun only lasts so long, Demos. What about children? What about when we're old? What about when I'm not interesting any more?'

A smile tugged on the corner of his mouth. 'Is that what you're afraid of? That I'll lose interest?'

'I'm not afraid of anything,' Althea snapped, exasperated. 'I'm just saying—'

'Let's leave the future to itself.' Demos cut her off. 'The present is interesting enough.' He reached for her, his hands curling around her shoulders, drawing her slowly, inexorably, to him. She couldn't summon the energy to resist. She didn't even want to, she realised as he folded her in his arms, her cheek against his chest so she could hear his steady heartbeat. 'As for children—yes. One day. If you want them. And when we're old? I plan to have fun then, too.' He stroked her hair, her cheek, his fingers setting a shower of sparks through her senses. 'It can be good between us, Althea. We've both seen much, done much. And now, like one of those beautiful old boats back at Mikrolimani, we need a safe harbour to come home to.'

'How flattering,' Althea muttered, and Demos chuckled.

'If you understood how I felt about boats, then you'd know it was a compliment indeed.'

She remained in the comforting cradle of Demos's arms. Neither of them spoke. She felt safe, Althea realised with a pang of surprise. In Demos's arms she felt safe.

It was an incredible thought. It was a frightening thought.

After a moment he stepped back, tilted her chin up so their eyes met. 'Yes?' he said, and Althea knew there was only one answer.

'Yes,' she said.

# CHAPTER SIX

'YOU'RE what?' Iolanthe's mouth dropped open as she stared at Althea in the spacious dressing room of one of Kolonoki's top boutiques.

'I'm getting married.' Althea smiled at her friend's expression, and she felt a small, surprising bubble of excitement well up inside of her. It had been three days since she told Demos she would marry him, and although she still felt moments of apprehension, even terror, right now she was enjoying herself.

'To who?'

'It will be announced in the papers tomorrow,' Althea replied, 'but it's Demos Atrikes.'

'The old guy?'

'He's thirty-two—only nine years older than me,' Althea replied.

Iolanthe shook her head, and Althea knew what she meant. Demos seemed older than his years; but then, so did she. Or at least she felt it.

'I thought you and Angelos…' Iolanthe trailed off uncertainly. 'He said—'

Althea knew she did not want to hear any more of Angelos's dirty gossip. 'Angelos,' she said firmly, 'is a little boy.' She twirled around, the ivory silk sheath dress flaring out around her ankles. 'What do you think? Bridal enough?'

'That's your wedding dress?' Iolanthe yelped, and Althea

smiled. Her friend no doubt wanted a gown with a dozen ruffled petticoats and a twenty-foot train.

'It's a small wedding. We're marrying quietly.'

'Why?'

She'd thought of having a big society wedding; her father would have preferred it. He wanted to show the world how he had his daughter under control and cleaned up. Perhaps that was why she had refused. That and the fact that the last thing she wanted was hundreds of Athens's social snobs staring at her, whispering about her from behind their hands.

'Because I want to. And so does Demos.'

Demos had not actually offered an opinion on their wedding. He'd simply said they would be married in two weeks.

Her smile faltered, and in the mirror she saw her eyes become dark and wide. She knew why Demos wanted to marry so quickly. She knew what he wanted from her.

She'd refused to sleep with him before the wedding. Outdated—old-fashioned, perhaps—and he'd told her she could hardly argue that she wanted to be kept pure.

Her mouth twisted in acknowledgement. No, she wasn't pure. Still, she wasn't ready to give herself in that way yet. She wouldn't ever be—not really—but she could prepare. She could pretend.

And Demos had agreed because it had seemed like a game, a sensual promise of what was to come. And it was; it would be. She could give him what he wanted. She *would*.

Althea turned away from the mirror. Yes, she would hold up her side of the bargain in exchange for the promises and possibilities Demos could give her.

'I like it,' she said with bright determination. She turned to Iolanthe. 'Will you be my bridesmaid? You can pick out your own dress.'

Iolanthe perked up at that suggestion, and they both went out to the showroom to riffle through the racks of silks and satins.

'Ooh…look at this,' Iolanthe purred, holding up a skimpy cocktail dress in vivid purple.

'Io, this is a *wedding*,' Althea reminded her, and her friend gave a little giggle.

'I'll get it anyway, for clubbing.' She paused, the dress balled carelessly in one fist. 'You'll still go out with us, won't you, Althea? You're not going to become old and boring, are you?'

'Hardly,' Althea replied lightly, but in truth she didn't know what the future held. Would Demos still want to be a part of the club and party scene, with his wife by his side? Just how much did he expect from her?

With a little shiver she realised she was naively envisaging living quite apart from Demos. She imagined him busy with his yachts and designs; she could do what she wanted, outside of the bedroom.

But what if she couldn't? What if Demos wanted more than just her body? What if he demanded her soul as well? Her time, her talents, *everything*? Wasn't that what marriage was supposed to be about?

Was that what Demos thought it was?

Just what, Althea wondered sickly, had she got herself into?

'Althea…' Iolanthe had picked another dress, this time a tea-length gown in pale green silk. 'Do you love him?' She sounded curious, and a little bit wistful.

Althea shook off her fears and gave her friend a brittle smile. She was being ridiculous; this was the twenty-first century. Marriage was not the end of her freedom. It was the beginning. At least it could be. 'Of course I don't love him,' she said. 'I barely know him. And I don't plan on loving anybody. I just want to have a good time.' She moved away to another rack, searching mindlessly through the rainbow of colours. She didn't want any more questions, couldn't give any more answers.

There would be no love in this marriage. Not now, not ever. Demos had made his intentions clear, and Althea knew herself well enough to know she was utterly incapable of love.

* * *

Ten days later Althea stood in her bedroom, the silk sheath she'd bought at the boutique now smoothed over her hips. It had two thin straps at each shoulder, threaded with gold shot-silk. It was a simple and elegant dress, classic and refined. She wondered what Demos would think when he saw her in it, and then asked herself why it mattered.

In the two weeks since they'd sealed their engagement with that kiss on his yacht, she'd only seen Demos a handful of times. He'd been busy with work—so much so that he'd had to cancel the dinner he'd arranged for them to have with his family.

Althea had been surprised by this abrupt shift in plans, but also grateful. The more Demos kept his distance the more she was able to believe in the fairy tale she'd spun for herself. The one where he left her alone. Her own private happily-ever-after.

Except he wouldn't leave her alone—not tonight. Not when they would be married, with no more excuses. Althea lifted her chin. She'd keep her side of the bargain. She'd play the part Demos wanted her to—the part he thought wasn't a role but her real self.

And perhaps it was. She'd played it for so long it felt real sometimes. Horrifyingly, numbingly real.

'Althea?' Iolanthe slipped into her bedroom, dressed in the gown she'd selected in the shop. 'The car is here to take you to the church.'

Althea nodded. 'I'm ready.'

'Are you?' Iolanthe tilted her head, a look of frank scepticism in her eyes. 'This has all happened so quickly. Are you sure you know what you're doing?'

No. She had absolutely no idea what she was doing, or even why she was doing it.

'Althea?'

Althea smiled. 'I'm getting married, Io,' she said, and her voice sounded careless. Carefree. 'That's what I'm doing.'

With a swish of her skirt she left the room. Outside, a car idled at the kerb. Spiros stood by the door.

'You're ready?' His voice was terse, and he fiddled with his tie. He was nervous, Althea realised. Did he think she was going to make some sort of scene?

She slipped into the car. It was too late for scenes, or for escapes. No—when it came to the final moment, the moment of surrender, she would be silent. Still. Waiting for it to be over. She was good at that.

Spiros slid in next to her, and Iolanthe sat in the front. The car pulled away from the kerb and Althea swallowed hard against a sudden flutter of nerves. It was too *late*.

It was only a few minutes' drive to the church, but it seemed far too long—and yet not nearly long enough. Strange, Althea thought distantly, how time did that; it slowed and sped all at once, so you wanted to wait for ever and yet you wanted to hurry. To go forward and go back at the same time. But only one was possible. There was only way forward now, and it led towards marriage. Towards Demos.

Spiros tapped a staccato rhythm against the door-frame, his gaze averted from hers. The mood in the car was sombre, as if they were on their way to a dirge rather than a wedding. Iolanthe's flirtatious banter with the driver was a background buzz of noise, and completely at odds with what Althea was feeling: uncertainty and dread, and underneath that the emotion she'd held at bay for so long. Fear. Raw, choking, terrible fear.

She was scared. Scared of marriage, of Demos, of what he expected of her. Scared, right now, of life itself. She swallowed the metallic tang of fear, heavy on her tongue, and closed her eyes, summoning strength from the last of her drained reserves.

She could get through this. She had to. Like everything else, she would glide through it, a smile on her lips, her mind and body disconnected…

And, as if a switch had been flipped in her head and heart, Althea slid blessedly into numbness, and knew she could do it.

The car pulled up to the church—a small building with an ornate stone façade. A crowd of a dozen or so people were milling about by its wooden doors. Althea saw a handful of her father's business associates, an older woman with a dour-looking man and a pretty, bright-eyed daughter—and Demos.

He stood taller than anyone else, dressed in a dark suit, his expression appropriately sober, a distinguished-looking man in his sixties by his elbow.

He held a bouquet of flowers in his hand; tradition required that he hand her the bouquet as they walked into the church together.

There would be no vows, no promises spoken. Merely standing in church together was considered enough. It was rather ironic, Althea thought, that she could get married without saying a word. If her father had had his way she would have been married without knowing about it at all.

The car stopped, and Althea reached for the door handle.

'Althea.'

She tensed, turned. Her father's eyes were bright, too bright. She couldn't bear to see his tears and she looked away again, staring outside at the milling crowd, determined to stay numb.

'Althea,' he said again, and it sounded like a plea. 'I want you to be happy. I hope—I pray—that you will be. Demos is a good man.'

'How would you know?' she asked. 'You barely know him.'

'I'm sorry,' her father said, and his voice was little more than a whisper. 'For whatever I've done that has made you so angry with me.'

Althea bit her lip, hard, and shook her head. She couldn't face her father now, and she certainly couldn't face the past. Not now, when her hold on her own composure was so tenuous and uncertain, when the prospect of walking up the steps and joining Demos at the church door seemed utterly daunting.

'I can't talk about this now,' she said, and her voice came out flat and cold. 'I'm about to get married.' She opened the door, then paused and turned around to gaze at him directly, even though it hurt her to see him so forlorn and wretched. 'I'm sorry too, Father, but it isn't enough.'

Demos smiled when he saw her emerge from the car,

although the smile died from his lips and his eyes as he took in her appearance, and Althea knew he was wondering what had just happened, what she was feeling, fearing.

She lifted her chin and smiled back, murmuring greetings to those in the crowd she knew before she reached Demos's side.

He presented her with the bouquet of purple stasis, his fingers wrapping around hers as he handed her the flowers. 'All right?' he murmured, so only she could hear.

Althea felt as if her life was being torn to shreds, her emotions flayed open, her body becoming a sacrifice. She was not remotely all right. She gave Demos and everyone around him a dazzling smile. 'Of course I am.'

And then they went into the church.

She didn't remember any of the service; it was a monotonous blur of words. She felt the ring slide onto her finger, then it was swapped three times with Demos's, in the church's tradition. She heard the prayers, the blessings, then felt the *stefana*, the crown symbolising the glory and honour that marriage brought, laid on her head.

The priest spoke again, and Demos held out his hand. Althea laid her own hand limply in his, felt his fingers close around hers, squeezing, strengthening. She looked up and saw something in Demos's eyes that she didn't expect: a flicker of fear.

And then it was gone, and she wondered if it had ever been there at all. Perhaps she had imagined it because she felt it herself.

They drank from the communion cup, and then the priest led them around the altar three times. Then it was finished. They were married. Althea gazed down at the heavy platinum ring on her finger and felt its weight in every ounce of her being.

Married. For better, for worse. For ever.

Cheers and congratulations erupted among the crowd, and Althea watched as the stout woman in black embraced Demos. He ushered her over, a curious mix of affection, exasperation and something darker warring across his features. 'Althea, my mother—Nerissa Leikos.'

'We are so happy!' Nerissa seized Althea and kissed both her cheeks. 'We have wanted Demos to marry for so long— and to such a beautiful girl... Your children will be beautiful too, and many!'

Althea smiled faintly, unable to wrap her head around that concept. Children. Many.

Her mind skittered away. She saw the young girl, pretty and pale-haired, standing on Demos's other side, and realised this must be his sister.

She knew so little about him, she thought, it was really rather appalling. How could you marry someone and not know his family? Whether he had a family? Although it seemed now that Demos did.

'You're Demos's sister?' she said, moving to chat with the younger girl while Demos exchanged greetings with his mother.

'Yes—Brianna.' The girl gazed at her with frank envy. 'I never thought Demos would marry. Do you love each other very much? You must to have married so quickly!' Her eyes widened, rounded. 'Or are you—?'

'No,' Althea said quickly, 'nothing like that.'

Brianna nodded. 'I didn't think so.' She paused, and there was a distant shadow in her eyes, a lurking fear that Althea saw and recognised because she knew how it looked. She knew how it felt. 'Do you think,' Brianna asked, her voice soft, small, 'that you'll like being married? Very much?'

'I hope so,' Althea said, with as much honesty as she could afford to reveal. 'I wouldn't have married otherwise.' That, she knew, was not necessarily honest, but she wasn't willing to reveal any more to a stranger—not even one as young and candid as Brianna.

'I never thought Demos would marry,' Brianna said, and she sounded disappointed. Hurt, even. 'He always told me he wouldn't. He *promised*...' She bit her lip, and Althea felt a frisson of alarm at the telltale sheen in her eyes. 'I thought he'd be there for me,' she said, almost to herself.

'And he will be,' Althea said. 'Our home will be open to you always, Brianna.' She meant the words, yet they sounded false. They felt false. What home? She'd never seen Demos's apartment, didn't know where they would be living.

It was all so very, very silly, she thought, how little she knew. Silly and sad.

'Are you ready?' Demos asked, his hand on her elbow. 'A car awaits to take us to the wedding breakfast.'

Althea nodded. No expense had been spared for the intimate but extravagant reception at one of Athens's best hotels. It was her father's way of showing her off, Althea knew. Showing that he'd got her married, just as he'd said he would.

Demos led her through the crowd to a dark-windowed sedan outside. Althea slipped into the leather interior and laid her head against the seat, exhausted. Overwhelmed. And, she acknowledged, her eyes closed, she didn't want to talk to Demos. She didn't even know what to say.

Fortunately he didn't speak, and when she dared to gaze at him from underneath her lids he looked grim, his hand rubbing his jaw in a preoccupied manner, his eyes on the blurred landscape outside.

'Here we are.'

The car stopped outside the King George Palace Hotel, and a doorman swept to open the car door. Althea let herself be guided out of the car, up the steps, and into the ornate lobby, with its famed marble carpet, scattered with crushed velvet sofas and gilt chairs.

Demos led her to a private banquet room for their wedding reception, and she stopped outside the doors, glimpsed the guests within and felt her stomach lurch violently, her control starting to slip away once more.

'I can't.'

Next to her, Demos stiffened. 'What do you mean, you can't?'

'I can't go in there.' She couldn't face the crowds, the chatting and laughter, the parody of happiness and love. She couldn't pretend for another minute—not when her nerves were screaming, crying out for a moment's respite.

Not when she was so tired of being someone else.

'Althea, this is your wedding. *Our* wedding.' Impatience and incredulity roughened Demos's tone. 'Why can't you go into a party and have a good time? Isn't that your speciality?' There was a slight sneer to his voice that made Althea cringe. 'Isn't that the kind of girl I married?'

She glanced up at him, her eyes wide, his words penetrating. His own face looked harsh, and so very unfamiliar. How could she have forgotten for a moment—a single second—that Demos believed he was marrying Althea Paranoussis, party girl extraordinaire? He'd said she was different, but not that different. Not too different.

And he? He wasn't different at all. The realisation echoed sickly through her. She'd wanted him to be different. She'd been *hoping*.

Yet now, as he shifted his weight with ill-concealed irritation, those barely articulated dreams died a quick and merciless death.

'Althea…' Demos said. The word was a warning, and she looked down, nodded in understanding and acceptance.

She took a second—a breath—and looked up, a dazzling smile pasted on her face, her eyes glittering. 'Of course that's the girl you married,' she said, and swept past him into the reception room.

The next few hours passed in a blur. Althea moved through the sumptuous room, with its frescoed walls and gilt chairs; she laughed, chatted, flirted. She drank champagne, clinking her glass in toast after meaningless toast. She even kissed Demos when someone demanded the couple do so, yet she barely felt his lips on hers. She barely felt anything at all.

It was so much easier, she thought, with a placidity drawn from numbness, not to feel anything. Not to care. Not to hurt.

Not to love, not to hate.

To feel nothing. Just…nothing.

The photographs had been taken, the dessert had been served, and the last rays of sunlight were slanting across the parquet floor when Demos sat next to her and murmured in her ear, 'It is time for us to go.'

Althea felt a single stab of terror before she slid once more into the comforting blanket of numbness. She nodded. 'Yes, I suppose it is.'

They said their goodbyes amidst a host of good wishes, embraces, kisses, bawdy jokes; all of them were meaningless words and gestures as Althea moved through it, indifferent, invisible.

She followed Demos from the reception to the hotel room he'd booked upstairs for tonight. Their wedding night.

They didn't speak in the elevator; Althea was dimly aware that Demos was tense, perhaps angry. She stood next to him and watched the lights blink on and off, the marble-tiled elevator rising higher and higher still, to the penthouse.

They entered the suite, and Althea moved through the luxurious rooms, noticing the silks, the satin and brocade, the original paintings adorning the walls in their heavy gold frames, the champagne chilling in a bucket by the balcony. From the window she saw the Parthenon, lit by the last rays of the sun before it sank beyond the horizon, before darkness came.

It was beautiful, gorgeous—oppressive. She felt the weight of that room and its expectations like a physical thing, burdening her, crippling her. She bowed beneath it.

'What the hell is wrong with you?'

Althea turned slowly from the window. Demos stood in the middle of the room; he'd shed his jacket and loosened his tie. He looked beautiful, virile—and utterly furious.

'Nothing's wrong with me,' she said after a moment, and her voice sounded tinny and strange to her own ears.

'You've been acting like a ghost since we married,' Demos

accused. 'Like a *zombie*. Did I marry a woman, Althea, or a shell?' He raked a hand through his hair. 'What's *happened* to you?'

It was a question she had no intention of answering. 'I'm tired,' she said stiffly. 'It's been a rather long day.'

Demos shook his head. 'I'm not accepting that. You party hard all day and night for weeks on end and *now* you're tired? That won't cut it, Althea. Not with me.'

She lifted her chin, her eyes snapping. 'I didn't realise one of the many requirements of being your wife was that I be the life of every party.'

'I said socially competent,' Demos replied, his tone chilly. 'And this wasn't *every party*, it was your wedding reception. *Our* wedding reception.' He took a step towards her, his face still dark with anger, his eyes glittering.

'Celebrating what?' she snapped back, goaded past endurance, her nerves fraying and ready to split. 'The loveless union of two strangers?'

'Don't throw that at me now,' Demos warned. 'You agreed. You knew what you were getting into.'

'That doesn't mean I have to like it!' Althea hissed, and his eyes darkened ominously.

'It would *help*,' he snarled.

Althea was stung to reply, 'Well, it's too late to back out now, if that's what you're thinking.'

He smiled; she didn't like it—the way his mouth curled upwards and his eyes moved over her. She was still dressed in her wedding finery, although she felt as if he were stripping her bare.

'Yes, it's too late,' he agreed, his voice pitched low, a parody of pleasantness. 'No one's going to back out now.'

Althea felt the breath freeze in her lungs, the brief streak of self-righteous indignation trickle away. She knew what he meant. She'd been preparing for this moment. The inevitable, of course, had to happen. Yet she wished it hadn't sprung from anger and accusation. The tension was still vibrating between them. She lifted her chin and even managed a smile. 'What are you saying?'

Demos's smile widened, although his eyes stayed hard and unforgiving. 'I want my wedding night.'

It was crude, blatant, and she hadn't expected it from him. Still, she was ready. 'I'll get changed,' she said with a hard, little smile, and Demos watched her carefully, his eyes flickering over her appearance, lingering on her face for so long that Althea wondered if her every emotion—every fear—could somehow be seen there.

'Good,' he said, and moved away towards the bar.

Althea went to the separate bedroom. The space was dominated by a king-sized bed with a coverlet of ivory satin. Someone had deposited her bags by the foot of the bed, and she riffled mindlessly through the contents Iolanthe had insisted on packing for her. She had a nightdress; Iolanthe had made sure of that. Except it wasn't a nightdress, she realised. It was a teddy.

She held up the scrap of black lace with a shudder. It was tiny, with several straps and buckles so she wasn't even sure how to put it on—not that she'd be wearing it. She balled it into her fist just as Demos came into the room.

He lounged in the doorway, one shoulder propped against the frame. He'd unbuttoned the top two buttons of his shirt, and he held a tumbler of whisky in one hand.

'You're acting awfully nervous, Elpis,' he said in a lazy voice she didn't like. 'Almost like a shy virgin. But I know you can't be one...can you?'

Althea stuffed the teddy back in her suitcase. 'No,' she said with a brittle little laugh, 'I'm not a virgin.'

'Good.'

She glanced back at him, an eyebrow arched. 'Most men would be disappointed, even if their modern sensibilities refused to allow them to admit it.'

'I'm not most men. I don't want a shy, scared innocent. I want a woman who knows how to give and receive pleasure.' He moved closer, leaving his tumbler on the bureau before he came over to her. He dropped his hands onto her shoulders and slid them over the silk of her dress, pushing the skinny straps away. 'That's why I chose you.'

His hands burned on her bare skin; it was not an altogether unpleasant feeling, but it still made alarm leap in her chest. She pushed it down, forcing the fear, the memories away as she always had done. 'A daring man,' she murmured, lifting her hands to lay them lightly on his chest, 'to be assured of such things without having sampled them.'

'I intend to sample them now,' Demos murmured. Yet he didn't move; he waited. Waited, Althea knew, for her to act. To show him just what kind of woman she was.

She could feel his heart beating against her palm, and carefully she smoothed her hands along the broad planes of his chest, her fingernails snagging on the buttons. Demos chuckled and, swallowing, forcing a little smile, she began to unbutton his shirt. His chest, she saw, was brown, beautiful, covered lightly with hair. Her fingers trembled just a little bit as she reached the last button and pushed the shirt back off his shoulders. He shrugged the rest of the way out.

Althea drew a fingertip along the long faded scar on his torso. Demos shuddered lightly under her touch. 'Where did you get that?'

'Knife fight.'

Her eyes widened. 'Really?'

'No.' He chuckled, capturing her hand and bringing it to his lips. 'A fish hook, actually. I was being stupid and fooling around on a boat.' Still smiling, he reached to the back of the dress and pulled the zipper down in one long, fluid moment. 'I've wanted to see you for so long.' The dress fell away, leaving her in only her bra, panties and stockings. It was, Althea thought dimly, almost worse than being naked. She stood there, utterly still, while Demos's gaze roved over her, lingering and caressing, and he smiled. 'You're beautiful.'

Beautiful. The word churned memories inside her, and she

orced herself to push them down. She could do this. She'd done
his before.

'Touch me,' Demos commanded, and under the order she
heard a surprising plea.

Althea lifted one hand, trailed it lightly down his chest, hot
skin over hard muscle. Her fingers halted at his belt buckle,
hesitating at the obvious sign of his arousal. She knew she
should be bold, shameless, and yet was utterly unable to be.

She hadn't expected this seduction—hadn't expected Demos
to want her to touch him, tease him. This kind of love-play, she
realised, wasn't in her realm of experience. The men she'd
been with didn't care about her own reaction or pleasure; they
were too intent on their own. She had no idea what to do.

She looked up at him, saw his eyes darken, and wondered
if she could go on. If she even knew how. 'Now you touch me,'
she said, her voice little more than a thread of sound, and
Demos smiled and picked her up.

She felt like a doll in his arms, all awkward angles and
lifeless limbs as he laid her on the bed.

He lay next to her, one arm cradling her head, his other
hand free to drift across her breasts, down her stomach to her
thighs. Althea shivered, and Demos must have taken it for a sign
of pleasure for he lowered his head and kissed her.

Somewhere deep inside Althea felt a startling jolt of pleasure,
a shock to her numb senses. She rested her hands on Demos's
back, glided them over his powerful shoulders—and lay still.

If she were still, like a good girl, it would be over so much
sooner. She closed her eyes.

Demos kissed her again, and she felt his fingers on her thigh,
teasing, stroking, getting closer. She tensed instinctively, then
forced herself to relax. She had to relax. She had to be still.

Her eyes were closed, her legs tense, yet parted, her body
still. Demos's fingers brushed her, seeking, and her legs closed
like two bands of iron in a helpless instinctive response. She
forced herself to open them, to lie passively underneath him.

Soon, she told herself. It would be over soon.

'Look at me.' Demos touched her eyelids with his fingers. 'Open your eyes, Althea. Look at me.'

Reluctantly her eyelids fluttered open, and she saw Demos gazing down at her with an intensity that unnerved her. He was so close, his body nearly on top of hers, and she could feel the length of his arousal jabbing against her middle. She gave an inadvertent frightened little gasp and clenched her eyes shut once more.

Muttering a curse, Demos rolled off her. She opened her eyes cautiously and saw he was sitting on the edge of the bed, his back to her, one hand raked through his hair. Althea lay there, clad only in her underwear, and waited.

'What is wrong with you?' Demos asked in a low, savage voice.

She fought the urge to cover herself and bunched her hands on the coverlet by her sides. 'I don't know what you mean.'

His back was still to her, every muscle and sinew quivering with tension. With anger. 'Were you raped?' he asked quietly. 'Is that it?'

'No—' It came out in an outraged breath, stunned as she was by the question—stunned and scared.

'Then why,' Demos asked, his voice hard and brutal, 'did I feel like I was forcing you just now?'

'What?' Althea blinked and scooted up to a sitting position. 'What?' she said again, her mind spinning, uncomprehending.

Demos turned around. He wore only his trousers, his hair dishevelled and his eyes burning with fury. 'This is not how I imagined this night to be,' he said, and Althea cringed, knowing what he meant.

This was not how he'd imagined his bride to be.

Muttering another curse, he stalked out of the bedroom. Althea heard the sliding glass door open and close, and knew he'd gone out on the terrace.

She slid back down the bed, drawing her knees up to her

chest as a matter of habit, in comfort. Her arms curled around her legs and she tucked her head down low, closing her eyes, clenching them shut.

This was such a mistake.

Had she actually thought she could fool Demos? That somehow he would continue to believe she was what she told the world she was even as she tried to be something different, to be *herself*?

It was impossible; she should have seen that. She should have realised that she couldn't keep up the charade—not even for one night, one *moment*. She didn't even want to.

And that, she thought grimly—sadly, even—was the problem. *Demos* wanted her to; he didn't even want it to be charade.

She'd deceived him by marrying him and she hadn't even realised it.

A police siren began its lonely wail on the street nine storeys below, and Demos tracked the blue blur of its light with a grim focus. Someone, somewhere, was in trouble, and dimly he wondered what it was. A death? A murder? An accident? Or just some drunk making a spectacle of himself?

He didn't know what crime had been committed in the seething city below, and he wasn't sure what had happened here either.

He shook his head slowly, remembering the feel of Althea's skin, the taste of her lips, the gentle trembling he'd taken for desire. Now he knew it for fear.

Fear. Althea Paranoussis—the woman whose name the tabloids delighted in smearing across their pages, the woman whom half the men at the club boasted about, the enchantress he'd been certain was sexy, sensual, a confident mistress of the bedroom—had been afraid. Of him. Of sex. Of sex with him.

He wondered now if she was really any of those things he'd so blithely thought. Sexy. Sensual. Experienced, even. Had he just been deceiving himself? Seeing what he wanted to see? Believing what he wanted to believe? He'd wanted Althea from the moment he saw her; even now, when she'd rejected him in nearly every way possible, he still did.

He'd convinced himself that the pieces had all fallen into place: his own sense of *ennui*, his sister's dependence, Althea's need for a husband. All had been pointing to marriage—simple, satisfying, sensual.

Yet now Demos wondered if they'd fallen into place or if he had simply jerked and shoved them till they fitted.

Because he'd convinced himself it was what he wanted. What he needed.

And now they didn't fit; nothing did. It was his wedding night—his *wedding* night—and he stood here alone, seething with frustration, confusion and unfulfilled desire. It was a potent mix.

Across from him the Parthenon cast a pearly sheen from its spotlight, elegant, eternal. His fist clenched on the railing and he swore again. Loudly.

What was wrong with Althea? Had she simply had a bad experience with a man? Did she not desire him? Was she playing a game, an expert and merciless tease even now?

He didn't know, and he didn't even want to guess. Flames of rage licked at his insides, tormenting, burning, and underneath was a far more dangerous flicker of an emotion Demos wouldn't, *couldn't* acknowledge.

With a grimace of disgust at himself and his own actions he turned away from the railing and headed inside for the bar. It was, he realised grimly, going to be a long, lonely night.

# CHAPTER SEVEN

ALTHEA awoke to discover she was alone, Demos's side of the bed still untouched. Sunlight streamed in from the wide windows, bathing the room in warm golden light.

She still wore only her underwear and stockings; she'd been too exhausted and demoralised to change. She lay unmoving in the bed and listened.

The suite was silent, and it gave her a sense of foreboding. Where was Demos? Had he left? If he had, she didn't know whether to be relieved or disappointed. She didn't know what to feel.

She swung her legs out of the bed and moved to her suitcase. Iolanthe had packed her sexiest, tartiest clothes: skimpy dresses and tank tops, low-cut jeans and mini-skirts. Grimacing, Althea pushed one garment aside after the other, a small, separate part of her surprised that she now refused to wear the wardrobe she'd determinedly revelled in for years.

She finally settled on the least revealing outfit: a pair of jeans and a cashmere sweater.

As she finished dressing she heard the quiet clink of china from the dining room, and she moved through the suite carefully, coming to a halt when she saw Demos at the table by the terrace, now laid for breakfast.

She didn't make a sound, but he still sensed her presence,

for he turned and with a neutral smile that didn't remotely reach his eyes gestured to the seat across from him.

'Come—have breakfast.'

Her stomach growled in response and she realised she'd barely eaten anything yesterday. Althea sat down across from him and Demos poured her some coffee.

'Sleep well?' he asked, his face, his voice still neutral.

Althea glanced up and saw something in his eyes—something dark and hard and unwelcome. She swallowed.

'No.'

'Neither did I.' They were both silent, the room heavy with an unspoken expectancy. 'What we need,' Demos said after a moment as he handed her a basket of *kolonokai*, 'is a honeymoon.'

Althea nearly spluttered her coffee. 'A *honeymoon*?'

'Yes,' Demos replied. 'I think we've both made some assumptions—some errors, even—about this marriage. About who we are.' He paused, and Althea swallowed again, setting her coffee cup down with an unsteady clatter. 'Some time away from the distractions and enticements of Athens, of our regular lives, could allow us get to know each other.' He paused again, and when he spoke this time it was with a new, deeper flintiness. 'Start over again.'

'Demos...' Althea wet her lips. 'I'm sorry about last night.'

'Are you?' He turned a page of his newspaper, not meeting her eyes. 'Care to elaborate?'

'I...' She closed her eyes, summoning strength. 'I was nervous,' she finally said. It was the truth—if only a small part of it. 'No matter what you've heard or read about me, I'm not used to tumbling into bed with men I barely know—'

'Funny, then, how you like to give that impression.' He pushed the paper away, his voice hardening. 'And is that what I am, Althea? A man you barely know?'

'We've only known each other a few weeks, Demos,' she replied, stung into strength once more. 'Be fair—'

'Fair? *Fair?*' His voice rose in incredulity, and he shook his head. 'Fair implies being *honest.*'

'I never lied to you.'

He shook his head, his expression turning blank once more—blank and yet resigned. 'It doesn't matter now. We're married, and we are not going to undo it.' He rose, tossing his napkin onto the table. 'We leave in an hour.'

'From the hotel? I don't—'

'We can buy whatever you need,' Demos replied with a shrug of dismissal, indifference. He paused, and a new bleakness entered his eyes, wrapped around Althea's soul. 'We need to get away from here, Althea. From the past, from *us.*'

She blinked. *Away. Escape.* 'Where are we going?'

'Kea. It's a remote island, although surprisingly near to Athens for all that. I have a villa there. We can be alone. We can...' his mouth hardened into a grim line before he turned away from her '...learn all we need to know about each other.'

And with that dire pronouncement he left the room.

It only took her a few minutes to finish breakfast as her appetite had vanished. She ate a few tasteless mouthfuls before pushing it away. Demos had set up his laptop in the lounge and was immersed in business, cradling his mobile to his ear as he typed on the keyboard. Althea looked at him for a moment—the slightly crooked nose, the strong line of his jaw, the look of utter determination darkening his eyes—and with a lurch wondered just what kind of marriage they could ever have.

Marriage. She was actually married to this man. She'd given a lifetime commitment based on a few paltry promises and a desperate desire to escape. To be free.

Shaking her head at her own inexcusable folly—blindness—she retreated into the bedroom and stuffed her scattered inappropriate clothes back into the suitcase. She glanced in the mirror, saw her face was pale, her eyes wide and frightened, and felt a stab of annoyance.

She was stronger than this. She could be stronger than this.

She'd endured so much more and she'd survived. She was here. She was healthy and whole, if not happy.

And perhaps even now she could be happy. For a tiny traitorous second she considered telling Demos what he'd demanded...*all he needed to know*. Then she shook her head, resolute. Where to begin? What to say? Who to believe?

No, the past was buried. Buried and—as best as it could be—forgotten.

She didn't want to remember. Certainly didn't want to relive the bitter memories of her youth. Yet the memories had been crowding her since Demos had come into her life, and slid under her defences without even realising he was doing so, stirring up memories he didn't even know about.

*You're such a pretty girl. Be good now. Be good for me...*

Bile rose suddenly in her throat and she lurched towards the bathroom, dropping to her knees in front of the toilet as her stomach rebelled and heaved. Though nothing came up. There was nothing to come up; she was empty inside.

She knelt there, the tiles cold and hard under her knees, her hair hanging down, and felt utterly wretched and alone.

'Althea?'

She looked up and saw Demos standing in the doorway, watching her with a hard, blank expression, his mouth tightening in what could only be distaste. She eased herself back, realising how desperate, how pathetic she must look.

'It's time to go,' he said. 'If you're ready.'

'Just...' She swallowed the acidic aftertaste and pushed her hair away from her face. 'Just give me a minute.'

Demos nodded, his eyes sweeping briefly over her dishevelled form, his mouth hardening into a grim line, and left the room.

Fifteen minutes later they were in his car, speeding along the Pan Tsaldari through Athens, heading for the harbour.

'I need to make a stop before we depart,' Demos said, his eyes on the road.

'Where?'

'My family.'

Althea's eyebrows rose. 'Why?'

He slid her a cool glance. 'You may not feel the need to speak to your own father, but I have obligations.' He paused, his eyes on the road, his fingers tightening on the wheel. 'Responsibilities.'

Althea pressed her lips together. 'Fine.'

Demos pushed harder on the accelerator and the car sped towards Piraeus.

They drove away from the harbour to the more crowded back streets, until they came to a street of squat cement houses, all framed with windowboxes of wilting begonias and twitching net curtains. Althea watched Demos's expression from the corner of her eye. His mouth had tightened, his eyes were shuttered, his body tense.

There were memories here.

'Do you want me to come in?'

Demos hesitated, and then gave a tiny shrug. 'I would hardly ask you to wait in the car, Althea. You're my *wife*.' He paused, adding reluctantly, 'This is the first time I've brought anyone here.' He sounded as if he regretted the decision to bring her.

Althea followed him down a concrete path to the front door as it was thrown open by the woman Althea had been introduced to yesterday: his mother Nerissa.

'Demos! We didn't expect to see you so soon!' Her wrinkled face was wreathed in smiles, although Althea thought she saw worry in her eyes…shadows. She waved him in with hurried shooing motions that still managed to be deferential. 'And your wife! Althea!' She embraced Althea, kissing her firmly on both cheeks. 'Come in—come in to the sitting room…'

Althea followed Demos into a small stuffy room, crowded with dark furniture and doilies.

'Sit,' Nerissa implored, sweeping off dustsheets and plumping cushions. 'Sit, please.'

Nerissa waited expectantly, hands folded across her middle, and Althea couldn't shake the feeling that the older woman was treating Demos as if he were a king from a distant, foreign, even vaguely hostile land.

Not her son.

'I would like to see Brianna,' Demos said, and Nerissa frowned, her gaze sliding nervously from his.

'Today isn't a good day, Demos. She's not herself…'

Demos swung around sharply. 'What do you mean, not herself?'

Nerissa shrugged, still not looking at him. 'The wedding yesterday was too much. So beautiful, of course, but for Brianna…' There was a suggestive lilt to her voice that Althea didn't understand.

'It upset her,' Demos stated flatly. 'I want to see her.' He stood in the middle of the room, dominating the space, looking utterly out of place. And yet, Althea realised, this was—or had once been—his home. His past. His *life*.

Nerissa sighed, clearly deferring to her son. 'As you wish. I will get us some coffee.' Althea rose to help, but Nerissa shooed her away. 'No, you must stay. You are a guest! Sit down—relax with my son.'

Nerissa left them alone, and the sofa creaked under their combined weight. Althea glanced around the dark, cramped little room, at the tottering end-tables crammed with lace doilies and cheaply framed photographs, the carefully arranged souvenir plates hanging on the wall. She glanced at Demos, felt his tension, and knew he was stifled by the smallness of the room, the life. Yet this was his family. His mother. His roots.

After a moment she heard the sound of footsteps on the stairs, and then the door was pushed open. Brianna stood there, her fair hair in a dishevelled cloud around her face, her eyes bright. She looked flushed, Althea saw, almost feverish, and her arms were crossed protectively over her body.

'Brianna.' Demos rose to embrace his sister. 'I didn't see you very much yesterday. I wanted to wish you well before I left—'

'You're leaving?' Brianna's shrill voice cut across him and Demos fell silent. 'You're leaving me?'

'Just for a week,' he said quietly. 'On my honeymoon.'

Her lip trembled and she pulled it almost viciously between her teeth. 'Don't.'

'I must,' Demos replied steadily. 'But when I return, Brianna, we can—'

'I hate you!'

Althea pressed back against the sofa, surprised by the viciousness of the sudden outburst. Brianna's whole body shook, her fists clenched at her sides.

'I hate you,' she said again, this time with a quiet force that was worse than her initial outburst.

Althea turned to glance at Demos, and shock streaked through her at the look of naked desolation on his face. It was a look she recognised, for she'd felt it herself. Despair. Guilt. Utter hopelessness. Then it was gone, replaced by a hardened implacability.

'Brianna,' Demos said after a moment, his voice quiet and strong, like a heartbeat, 'you know I love you.'

'No, you don't.' Brianna shook her head in one violent movement.

Althea could see she was losing her thin thread of control. She recognised the signs—had felt them herself.

'If you did, you never would have left me the first time. *Remember?*'

She spoke the single word so savagely that Althea flinched— and so, she saw, did Demos.

Brianna began to cry, suddenly and loudly—gulping, ugly sobs that filled the room with their harsh, guttural sound.

Demos moved to pull his sister into his arms and she went bonelessly into his embrace, curling into him like a child.

Althea felt like an intruder. She *was* an intruder—intruding on Demos's family, his time with his sister, a life she'd had no idea about. Reckless rich playboy. That was how she'd seen him, judged him.

*I think we've both made some assumptions—some errors, even—about this marriage. About who we are.*

'Excuse me,' she whispered, and left the room. The door closed with a soft click and Althea glanced at the dark, narrow corridor, wondering where to go. What to do.

Through the thin walls she heard Demos murmur soothingly to his sister, then Brianna sniffle and gulp and try to control her sobbing.

'Brianna, I didn't come here to upset you,' Demos said. 'I only wanted to see you, to assure you that I'd be back soon.'

'With *her*,' Brianna spat, and outside the room Althea stiffened.

'Yes, with her,' Demos replied. 'My wife. Brianna, one of the reasons I married was to offer you—'

'You'll forget all about me.' Brianna cut him off, her voice thick with tears. 'Like before. Even when you promised…'

'Never,' Demos replied, and though he spoke flatly Althea thought she could hear the ache of regret behind the word. Or perhaps she was just feeling it herself.

'Here we are,' Nerissa sang out, and Althea jumped away from the door.

'Lovely…' she murmured, her mind still spinning from the overheard conversation.

The rest of the visit passed in awkward conversation buoyed along by Nerissa's ebullience. She was clearly thrilled her son had finally married, and Althea supposed she'd never read the tabloids or heard of his bride's reputation. Brianna sat curled up in the corner, quiet and sulky, her speculative gaze flitting from Demos to Althea.

Finally, after an endless hour, they made their farewells. Demos didn't speak as he drove to the harbour. Althea didn't know what to say.

'Are we taking your boat?' she finally asked, as Mikrolimano came into view.

'Yes,' Demos replied shortly, and they didn't speak again until they were aboard the yacht, with Demos at the helm, guiding the craft out of the harbour.

It was a beautiful day. The sea sparkled blue-green under a cloudless sky, and the sun was warm and forgiving on Althea's bare arms. She stood at the railing, watching as the villas and tenements of Piraeus grew smaller, the yachts and fishing boats in the harbour becoming nothing more than a blur of white sails.

All around them the sea was open, endless, the gulf islands a grey-green smudge on the horizon.

Once they were out on the open sea Demos joined her at the rail. The fresh, salty sea breeze was blowing over them. A few clouds, fleecy and white, had formed on the horizon.

Althea had been lost in thought, her lip pulled between her teeth, but as Demos joined her she finally spoke. 'You didn't marry me to rescue me,' she said slowly, feeling each word, each realisation. 'You did it to rescue Brianna.'

Demos was silent, his gaze on that endless horizon, his face partially averted from hers. 'I'm not rescuing anyone,' he said after a long moment, his voice flat.

'What I don't understand,' she continued, 'is how marrying me—me, of all people—would help Brianna.' She paused, her gaze also on the sea, on the smudge of land on the horizon growing closer, darker. 'Marrying anyone, for that matter.'

Demos was silent for so long that Althea wondered if he was ever going to answer her. She wondered if their marriage would be anything more than a shell—a charade based on a carefully constructed labyrinth of lies and half-truths.

'My father left when Brianna was just a baby—only a year old,' he finally said. 'My sisters were at school, and then they married young. My mother worked at a laundry. I was left to take care of her, and sometimes it has seemed to Brianna that I'm all she's ever had.'

Althea digested this slowly; the truth was not so different from what she'd begun to suspect. 'So wouldn't your marrying someone make her jealous? I can't see how it would help.'

'I wanted to offer Brianna some stability,' Demos replied, and there was an implacable note to his tone. 'She looks to me as an example, and I decided it was time to give her a good one. Besides, if I marry perhaps she might too. She needs to be protected...provided for. As you could see, she's...' He paused, and Althea slid a sideways glance at him, saw the frown lines drawn from nose to mouth. He shook his head. 'Troubled.'

Brianna was more than simply troubled, Althea thought. She was unstable—ready to fall apart at any moment.

She'd known how that felt. She still did.

It shocked her, a sharp pain deep inside, to realise that no matter what façade she presented to the world—to Demos— she was still the girl she'd always been on the inside: frightened, desperate, alone. So sickeningly similar to Brianna.

Did you ever learn from your mistakes? Althea wondered. Did you ever get a chance to heal? Or did you just blunder on and on, coping, denying, existing as best as you could?

'Do you really think she's in any condition to be married?' she finally asked, and Demo's gaze narrowed.

'Are you?' he challenged coolly.

Althea felt colour rush to her face. *Was she?*

She turned away from the railing, from Demos, the sudden jumbled thoughts and memories too much for her, threatening to spill over as she could never let them.

She sucked in a shocked breath when Demos stayed her by taking hold of her wrist.

'Let me go—'

'Althea...' Whatever he'd been about to say died on his lips as he looked down at her arm. He'd gone utterly still, his face blank, and Althea followed his gaze to the line of faint, pale scars marring the tender skin of her inner elbow. They both stared down at the revealing marks for a long, suspended moment.

Althea tried to pull away, but he held fast, his grip gentle but firm. 'What's this?' he asked quietly.

She hesitated, thoughts and memories flashing through her so fast she could barely hold onto them. She didn't even want to. She hadn't looked at those scars, remembered them, in years. 'Schoolgirl stuff,' she finally said with a shrug.

'Schoolgirl?' Demos prompted, and there was a dark note in his voice that told Althea he would not be so easily dismissed.

'Boarding school,' she explained, trying to sound impatient, bored. 'You know—you slap someone's arm to see how much pain they can endure. The person who lasts the longest wins. Just pranks, really. That's all.'

'How much pain they can endure?' Demos repeated in a chilling murmur. He trailed one finger along those faint, damning lines and Althea felt as if he were marking her soul. 'But this isn't a slap on the arm,' he continued, his voice still soft, yet filled with a menacing knowledge. 'These are scars. And by their size and shape I'd guess they were caused by a razor.'

Again she tried to jerk her arm away; again he held on. Waiting. His eyes met hers, cold and grey and filled with a terrible knowledge. Power.

He knew what those scars meant, knew how they'd been caused, and though she hadn't even thought of them in years, suddenly it felt as if those scars provided Demos with a terrifying window into her soul. Into her heart. And she could tell by the dark flicker in his eyes that he didn't like what he saw.

'I told you—it was a long time ago,' she finally said, her lips and her mind numb. Numb, and yet not with the almost pleasant lack of sensation she'd drifted into during her wedding, her wedding night. No, this numbness was an urgent, desperate dam, holding back the tide of feeling, the memories, the fear, the anger and the shame. And she was suddenly afraid it was going to crack, a hairline fracture that would burst wide open.

'Why did you cut yourself?' Demos asked, and Althea tried to pull her arm away again. He held on.

She shrugged. 'It was a dare, I suppose—'

'No, it wasn't.' He cut her off, speaking with a firm decision that left her mouth gaping open and her mind reeling. 'My sister cut herself,' he continued in a voice of eerie, dispassionate calm. 'She was hospitalised for it when she was fourteen. She had marks on her arm just like this.'

'I never—' Althea began, but stopped when he shook his head.

'You know what she said? She said it helped her feel in control. In control of the pain.' He paused, his throat working, his expression shuttered. 'I never could understand that. But, tell me, is it true?' His gaze fastened on hers, unyielding. '*Do* you feel more in control when you harm yourself?'

Althea jerked hard and he let her go, making her take a few stumbling steps backwards. She opened her mouth. She meant to say that she wouldn't know, that it had just been a prank, as she'd said, but instead she found herself saying, in a flat, faraway voice, 'No. It didn't. At least, not after a little while.' She paused, curling her arm inwards, hiding the scars from his view, from her own. 'It was a relief right after. Then it stopped.'

She couldn't look at him; she'd never told anyone about those scars. No one had ever asked. No one had ever noticed. She waited, feeling exposed, vulnerable, and a little bit afraid.

'What happened?' Demos finally asked. 'What happened to you to make you cut yourself?'

He spoke heavily, as if he were disappointed. As if she had disappointed him. And Althea realised she had. He'd wanted to marry a sexually sophisticated, carefree, fun-loving party princess.

And he'd got her instead.

'Althea?' he prompted, and she realised she hadn't answered. Couldn't. She couldn't spill her sordid secrets to a man who hadn't asked for them, hadn't bargained on getting them.

Didn't want them.

'My mother died,' she finally said, her gaze sliding from his to rest once more on the hazy horizon, 'when I was thirteen. It was a difficult time for me.'

'I imagine it was,' Demos agreed after a moment. And Althea felt she hadn't fooled him at all. Yet he turned away to face the sea once more, and she took the opportunity to escape inside the cabin, to forget or at least to force down everything Demos had churned up within her.

Rage. He felt rage. Pure, unrelenting rage. Demos gripped the railing of the boat so his knuckles turned white and the bones of his hands ached.

He felt rage…at himself. He should have known. He could have guessed. Didn't he know the signs? Hadn't he *lived* them? Yet he'd let himself be convinced by Althea's fun-loving façade, determined she was shameless rather than shy. He'd wanted her—what he'd thought she promised—and so he'd pushed away any obstacles. Any warnings.

Now he remembered how she'd slipped away from Angelos's embrace that first night, almost as if she were frightened. How she'd jerked back when he touched her. Hell, she'd run out on *him* and he'd thought she was being provocative. *Flirting.*

He thought of how she'd kept telling him, *You don't know me.* And she'd been right. He hadn't known her.

Now he was afraid he did.

Now he saw the truth, stark as it was. What had happened to her to make her so afraid of sex? Of men? Of *life?* Or, he wondered grimly, the ragged edges of despair darkening his mind, was she just unstable?

Unstable. Unsafe. Rage and another more terrible emotion churned within him—an emotion he'd never wanted to feel again: fear. He closed his eyes.

It was likely, Demos realised, that Althea was just as damaged and dangerous as Brianna, who had endlessly needed him, whom he'd endlessly disappointed.

*Just as…* And he was married to her.

* * *

Althea didn't see Demos for the rest of the trip to Kea. She sat curled up on a leather divan, her mind seething with questions, memories. She wanted to choke them back down, but they kept rising—remnants of voices, feelings, thoughts that swirled through her mind like mocking ghosts, forcing her to confront what she'd held at bay for so long.

She *couldn't*. Not yet. Not ever.

'Mrs Atrikes?'

The name jerked her around and shock rippled through her. *Mrs Atrikes.*

Demos's assistant stood by the door to the galley, smiling at her look of surprise. 'It is still unfamiliar, yes?' he said with a chuckle, and Althea forced herself to smile. 'Would you like a cup of coffee?'

'Yes, thank you,' Althea said, and her smile turned genuine as she continued, 'I don't know your name.'

'Feodore.'

Her gaze took in his grey, grizzled appearance: a man who had seen and done much. 'How do you know Demos?'

Feodore's smile was tinged with sorrow. 'I worked with his father.'

She followed Feodore into the narrow galley and watched as he set about pouring water and spooning coffee granules into the *briki*. She leaned against the doorway. 'I know his father left when Demos was young. Where is he now?'

'Dead.'

There was so much that Demos hadn't mentioned, that either of them hadn't mentioned. She felt the weight of unspoken revelations and regrets pressing her down, squeezing her heart. 'Why did he leave?'

Feodore slotted her a glance that was both kindly and knowing. 'Shouldn't you ask Demos that?'

Althea smiled wryly. 'It's easier to ask you.'

Feodore was silent for a long moment, and Althea didn't think he was going to answer. 'He's a good man, Demos,' he finally said. A rich, dark foam rose in the *briki*, and Feodore carefully divided it between two cups, pouring the rest of the coffee on top. He handed a cup to Althea. 'His father left when he was only twelve, you know. It was a shameful thing.' Feodore shook his head in memory. 'He never wrote, never sent money. Nothing.'

Althea nodded, although there was still so much she didn't understand. 'What happened then?'

'Demos took responsibility for his family.'

She tried to imagine him, twelve years old, bearing the weight and responsibility of a man. 'Did you help him?' she asked, and Feodore gave a little shrug.

'As much as I could. But no one had much money. We were fishermen, and I took Demos onto my boat. He left at the end of the day with a handful of copper—not much to support his family on. And none of us had much more to offer. Nothing that Demos was willing to accept.' Feodore smiled suddenly, revealing strong, tobacco-stained teeth with a few gaps. 'But he worked hard, he supported his family, and he made himself the man he is today. And now look—he's hiring me, extending his hand to me.' He shook his head, this time with admiration. 'He is a good man.'

Althea nodded, her throat turning tight. A good man. Yes, she believed it. He'd been honest when she hadn't, and now she saw only his disappointment and regret. It was her own fault—her own blindness and belief that she could be what he wanted. That she was enough when she so obviously, so terribly, wasn't.

Could she ever be what Demos wanted? The question reverberated emptily through her mind.

She raised her cup of strong, steaming coffee. 'Thanks for this.' Feodore smiled, and Althea had a feeling he knew she'd been thanking him for more than the drink.

An hour later Demos guided the boat into the island's small harbour and docked. Althea stared out at a stretch of sandy beach framed by a concrete promenade lined with restaurants and shops. Above the town a ruined *acropolis* and an abandoned metal factory told their separate stories of the island's history.

Althea's gaze swept the lonely promenade—a few scattered tables, mostly empty. A couple of old women shuffled along, clutching their paper-wrapped purchases. It was a far cry from many of the more populated and visited islands, with their trendy bars and blaring music. Kea looked lonely, windswept, beautiful.

'It's the closest of the Cyclades to Athens, yet it has hardly any tourists,' Demos said.

Althea stiffened in surprise; he'd left the boat and joined her on the dock without her noticing.

'There's no ferry from Athens,' he explained. 'Although there probably will be one day.'

'And you have a villa here?'

'Yes—just over there.' He jerked a shoulder to the left, where the street wound towards the rocky cliff. 'We can go there now, rest and change, and then go out to dinner.'

They walked the length of the promenade while Feodore took their bags in a taxi. Demos pointed out a few shops, although Althea was barely listening. She made a pretence of nodding, murmuring, pretending as always.

They turned off the promenade onto a steep, narrow street that wound its way through whitewashed buildings up a rocky hill.

Althea felt a flicker of anticipation as they made the ascent, wondering what lay at their journey's end.

She was not disappointed. The street widened into a small courtyard framed by terracotta pots with trailing bougainvillaea, which led directly into Demos's villa—a sprawling, stucco building, with bright blue shutters, that looked almost as if it were formed from the rock on which its foundations had been laid.

The sun was hot on the bare hillside, and Althea turned around to face the sea in surprised appreciation. The town of Korissia lay before them, a gentle cluster of whitewashed buildings nestled in a curve of sand, stretching to the jewel-toned sea. The sight was so innately peaceful and calming, laid before her in such gracious simplicity, that she felt something—something she'd held so tightly—loosen and lighten within her.

'It's lovely,' she murmured, and Demos paused in the act of unlocking the door to flash her a quick smile.

'Yes…I chose it for the view alone.' He opened the door and ushered her inside.

The villa was decorated in comfortable luxury: leather sofas and scattered woven rugs on the terracotta-tiled floor. It had the air, Althea thought, of a place that had been unlived in for some time and quickly prepared for incoming guests.

She turned to Demos. 'Is no one here?'

'We are.'

'Yes, but you must have a housekeeper or a maid…'

'There's a woman from the village who comes in once a week.'

Demos continued watching her, smiling faintly but with his eyes narrowed, so that Althea was tempted to fidget. She didn't. 'What about Feodore?'

'He'll drop off our luggage and then return to Athens.'

'On your boat?'

'Yes. He'll return for us in a week.'

She was, she realised with a flash of something close to anger, a prisoner. And why? What could he want from her now? What could he hope to gain?

'You must be tired,' Demos said. 'Let me show you your room.'

'*My* room?' she repeated, and he didn't look back at her as he led the way up the stairs.

'Do you think I'm going to force myself on you?' he asked. 'Clearly you need some time before you feel comfortable enough to share your body with me.' Demos paused in the doorway of a room soothingly decorated in shades of blue and green. 'But when you are ready,' he said, and a steely note of certainty entered his voice, 'I will be waiting.'

He gestured for her to enter the room, and Althea paused on the threshold.

'Demos…perhaps this was a mistake.'

Demos smiled, his voice chillingly polite. 'To what are you referring?'

Althea opened her mouth; it hurt to put it so plainly. 'Our marriage. I'm not…I'm not the woman you thought I was.'

'Then the error is my own,' Demos replied, his voice still cool, 'and one I am prepared to live with.'

'But—'

'We will not talk of this again, Althea.' His hand closed on her wrist, turning her arm so the pale, faded scars were splayed to their view. 'You are my wife, Althea. My *wife*. Every part of you. I'm not going to run away from that, from my responsibility, simply because you have a bit more baggage than I anticipated.'

It should have made her feel better, and perhaps he'd meant it to, but instead she felt worse. As if she were nothing more to Demos than that baggage. His burden.

'And what,' she asked quietly, 'if I don't want to be your responsibility?'

'You have no choice.' Demos's teeth flashed in a smile of grim humour. 'Or rather, you made that choice when you made our marriage vows.'

'I didn't actually make any vows,' she reminded him.

'You stood next to me in church. You looked into my eyes.' There was a raw note in his voice that made Althea ache inside, in that forgotten place. 'You are my wife, Althea. And I am your husband. That means something to me. And it should mean something to you. Now, get some rest. We'll be going out for dinner tonight.'

Before she could frame a reply he'd left, releasing her wrist and disappearing downstairs.

Althea wandered around the room. The sea flashed brightly from the window as the sun sparkled and danced on its surface. She felt restless and anxious—and yet she was, she realised, exhausted, and so finally she kicked off her shoes and sank onto the bed, pulling the covers over her.

She awoke a few hours later. The sun was lower in the sky,

sending golden ripples over the sea outside. Her suitcase was now by the end of her bed, and she wondered if Demos had brought it in while she was asleep. He must have, she realised, for Feodore had returned to the mainland.

They were alone. Alone with their memories and their fears and their disappointments.

*Disappointment.* The word echoed remorselessly through her, and she drew her knees up against her chest, closing her eyes to will the memories, the feelings away.

They were too close, too much, hovering on the fringes of her consciousness, reflected in the dark flicker of Demos's eyes when he'd drawn a fingertip along those terrible, damning scars, causing the first hairline fracture in her composure. Her control.

A knock sounded on the door. 'Althea? Are you ready?'

Althea jerked upright and blinked the world back into focus. 'Yes…' Her voice came out in a croak. 'Just a moment.'

Demos was waiting in the lounge when she went downstairs, dressed casually in a grey polo shirt and dark trousers. He turned when he heard her, and for a second—no more—his eyes blazed into hers before he smiled and said, with a careless little shrug, 'Shall we?'

Althea nodded, and after a second's hesitation accepted his outstretched hand.

The sun was just disappearing beyond the horizon as they set out from the villa, down the narrow, steeply winding street. By the time they came out onto the promenade the sun had truly set and the sky was washed in violet. Boats bobbed gently in the dark silky water, and a few of the restaurants had fairy lights spangled over their awnings.

Demos chose a taverna in the middle of the street, and, as Althea had half expected, the proprietor came out and greeted him, kissing him on both cheeks.

Demos introduced her—'Althea—my wife'—to a clamour of cries and excited shouts. Althea was passed from person to person, hands clutching her shoulders, people kissing her cheeks and exclaiming over her beauty and charm.

She couldn't breathe.

She wasn't aware of the faces, their features; she couldn't focus, only feel. Feel the hands, the breath, the mouths.

She dragged in a laboured breath and saw spots dance before her eyes. This was ridiculous, she told herself; she could do this. These people were kind; they meant well. She hadn't acted like this in years—hadn't felt this fear so sharply in nearly a decade.

Yet marriage, Demos, *everything* that had happened in the last fortnight, now brought it all rushing back.

'Are you all right?' Demos murmured in her ear, and she heard the undercurrent of censure. She was not handling this well, and he could tell.

She pushed her hair away from her flushed face and nodded. 'Yes, I'm fine.' She turned to the crowd of people, each face wreathed in smiles, each voice bestowing only blessing, and found her voice.

'*Efharisto. Efharisto…*'

Finally they were alone at their own table, and Althea sank gratefully into her seat, hiding her face with the handwritten menu.

'That bothered you,' Demos observed, and she stared at the menu's offerings until the words blurred.

'It was a bit overwhelming,' she replied after a moment. 'It seems you're well known here. Well liked, too.'

Demos shrugged. 'I bought the villa here when I first made my money. I've known them a long time.'

She put the menu down, trusting herself now. 'Do you come here often?'

'As often as I can. I wanted to live here, but work has made it impossible thus far.'

'Has it? It didn't take long to get here by boat.'

'True.'

'You'd miss the evenings out, though, wouldn't you?' Althea guessed. 'The clubs, the parties…' The women. The affairs.

'I suppose I would have once,' Demos agreed. 'Not any more.'

'Why not?'

A look of irritation and impatience flickered across his features. 'Because I'm married, Althea. *We're* married.'

She turned back to her menu. 'Marriage surely doesn't preclude going out?'

'I hope you don't actually think,' he said, in a voice made all the more menacing by its quiet intent, 'to continue your antics when we return to Athens.'

'And just what "antics" are you referring to?'

Demos's eyes and voice were hard and flat. 'Carousing with the likes of Angelos Fotopoulos. Dancing, drinking with men like him—'

Althea let out a laugh of disbelief. 'You offered to marry me so I wouldn't have to deal with Angelos. Do you honestly think I want his company now?'

'You wanted his company the other night.'

'Actually, I didn't,' Althea replied tartly. She leaned forward, her hair swinging down to partly obscure her face. 'I can't believe you still think…' She paused, saw the tightness in his mouth, the hardness in his eyes. 'Are you *jealous*?' she asked in disbelief, and yet with a strange, inexplicable hope.

'I am not,' Demos assured her coolly. He tossed his napkin onto the table and made a sound of disgust deep in his throat. 'I don't know *what* to be, Althea,' he continued in a low voice. 'I don't know what kind of woman you are.'

She blinked, swallowed. 'No, you don't.'

'So tell me.'

She gave her head a little shake.

'You're hiding some secret,' Demos continued, his voice determined yet purposefully bland. 'Something that made you afraid of men. Of sex. Of me.'

'No—'

'Yes. What I don't understand is, if that is so, why did you go to clubs? Why did you sleep with the likes of Angelos and no doubt a dozen other men?' His voice intensified to a low, throbbing pitch. 'Why give yourself so cheaply to them and refuse *me*?'

Althea blinked back tears. *Tears*. She felt the sudden moisture with surprise. 'It's not like that.'

'Then tell me how it is.'

Her throat ached; her eyes stung. She opened her mouth, unsure what to say, how to begin—if she could. Then a hand clapped down on her shoulder.

'Where have you been keeping this beauty.'

Althea tensed under the onslaught of that firm hand, those fingers kneading her shoulder, close to her collarbone. She saw Demos's mouth thin, and she turned in her seat to see a beefy man in his fifties smiling jovially—although his eyes were small and beady, glittering with lascivious intent.

Or maybe she just thought they were. Maybe he was smiling with fatherly familiarity and she couldn't tell.

She couldn't tell anything any more.

'Hello, Esteban,' Demos said coolly. 'This is my wife— Althea.' He rose from the table, helping Althea to rise as well.

'She's lovely—a pearl beyond price,' Esteban said, and his eyes swept over her, lingering…or did they?

Was she imagining it? She felt as if the pieces of her world had tilted and slid and she couldn't put them back together. She didn't know what was happening. Not with Demos, not with this stranger. Not with herself.

Althea glanced at Demos; he looked implacable, unperturbed.

'Yes, she is,' he agreed, and his tone was a dismissal. Althea felt the first stirrings of relief.

'A kiss for the bride,' Esteban declared, his hands on her shoulders once more, drawing her closer.

Althea froze; she couldn't see Demos. She could only see— and feel—the hot breath of the man before her as his lips moved nearer to hers with undeniable intent. And suddenly, finally, she couldn't.

She couldn't be kissed by another man when she didn't want to be. She couldn't be kissed while Demos watched. Couldn't allow herself to be touched by this loathsome stranger. She wouldn't.

Finally she broke. Finally it was too much. And the realisation that finally all the tightly held pieces of herself were scattered and free was suddenly strangely a relief.

With a little cry she wrenched away, heard the ripple of surprise throughout the taverna and the tearing of her own dress as Esteban's fat fingers snagged on its buttons.

She saw Demos's eyes narrow, his expression like a steel trap, but she didn't care.

The hairline fracture in her composure, maintained all these years, had split wide open. She felt the carefully held pieces of herself breaking apart, scattering, shattering, and there was nothing she could do to stop it.

So she wouldn't.

She'd escape.

She turned, weaving her way through the tables, mindless of the whispers, the shouts, the knocked over chairs, the clatter of silverware. Nothing mattered but escape. Freedom.

She didn't know if Demos was behind her—if Esteban was—but she just kept going, out of the restaurant and down the promenade, into the star-strewn night.

# CHAPTER EIGHT

THERE was nowhere for her to go. Althea realised that as she ran to the only place she knew on this forsaken island: Demos's villa.

Her heels clattered on the concrete promenade and her hair flew out behind her in a dark stream. Her mind was a blur. She made her way up the narrow, winding street, her breath a ragged gasp in her chest.

Demos's villa loomed out of the darkness and she turned the knob, *praying*…

It was open. She slammed the door behind her and hurried up the stairs. She didn't know where she was going, what she was thinking…

Only feeling. *Feeling*. Hurt, memory, pain, sorrow.

Anger.

*Rage*.

It all came rushing, an endless river, and she couldn't stop it. For once she didn't even want to.

She found herself in the *en suite* bathroom, with its glossy tiles and fluffy towels, its wide window framing a view of the darkened sea. She turned the shower on full power, full heat, and stripped off her clothes.

She needed to be clean. Cleansed.

Althea stood underneath the steady spray and closed her eyes, took deep breaths of hot, muggy air. The water scalded her, soothed her.

It made her numb again. Almost.

Then the shower curtain was ripped away, and a scream caught in her throat as she flung her hands up to shield herself.

Demos stood there, his breathing ragged, his face darkly furious. 'Just what the hell do you think you're doing?' he demanded in a rasp, but Althea barely heard him.

'Get out!' It came out as a scream, torn from her soul. 'Get out, get out, get *out*!'

Demos ignored her. 'Why did you run out of the restaurant, Althea? Run out on me? What is—?'

'Get out!' She pounded slick wet fists against his chest, soaking his shirt. She was barely conscious of her own nakedness and vulnerability; the only desire coursing through her was to be alone. To be safe. 'Get out,' she demanded in a sob, and Demos caught her fists with his hands.

'You are my wife—' he began.

And the realisation that he believed that title allowed him licence, liberty, was more than she could bear.

'Then I don't want to be your wife!' she screamed. 'I don't want any part of you!' She pushed against him, flailing, furious, but he held onto her easily, and this only made her more angrier.

'You have no right...*no right*!' She was filled with a scalding anger that she'd never felt before—had never allowed herself to feel. Rage. Pure, strong, clean. She pushed against his chest, kicked his shins, panic and fury rising, choking her, but he was immovable. Unshakeable. A rock when she didn't want one. A prison when she craved freedom.

And in the midst of the chaos of her own actions she realised Demos was not defending himself. He'd stopped holding her; his hands were at his sides as he gave himself up to her anger, to her kicks and hits and screams.

Through a haze of angry tears she saw his face, and the look of desolate acceptance on his features shocked her.

He thought he deserved this. He looked, she realised, as if he blamed himself. As if this—*she*—was his fault.

Somehow that made her even more furious, more desperate. She wanted a reaction, a result. Some way to end this, to *feel*, to hurt *him*—

Then, even as her own anger spent itself, there emerged a detached, rational part of herself—a silent spectator who had observed her fighting and screeching as she never had before— as perhaps she should have—and now began to weep.

She hadn't cried since her mother died. Even then a part of her had known that to release the tears would be to open a door that perhaps could not be closed again, to acknowledge emotions her childish heart had no way of dealing with. That door had stayed firmly, cleverly shut.

Now it burst open, blew apart, and the tears came. First just silent streaks down her face, then louder, larger, an outpouring of emotion that she no longer had the power to check.

She couldn't see Demos's expression through the haze of her tears, and she was glad. She'd never cried like this—big, tearing gulps, her body racked with sobs. She sank to her knees, her arms curling around her body, her head bowed, her wet hair trailing the floor.

She didn't even try to stop. She couldn't. She let her face, her body, be washed by the tide of sorrow, let each sob be chased by yet another, rising from a deep and endless well within her.

Demos stood there watching her, unmoving, and Althea was barely aware of him, her own misery too much to bear.

She didn't know how long she cried. She didn't know how many tears she had. After a while the room was silent except for her own ragged breathing. She felt exhausted. Sated.

It wasn't, she realised distantly, a bad feeling.

Yet she couldn't look at Demos—couldn't bear to see the expression on his face even though she had no idea how he would feel. What he thought.

Demos turned off the shower. Still Althea wouldn't look at him. She heard him move, then felt him drape a thick towel around her still-wet shoulders.

He reached for her hand, and she followed him numbly back to her bedroom. By the side of the bed he dried her off, as if she were a child, rubbing her bare limbs with brisk movements. He slid a soft cotton shirt of his own over her; it hung down to her knees. Then he pulled back the covers and she slipped underneath the duvet, curling into a ball, still not looking at him.

After a moment he left, and Althea closed her eyes, too exhausted and overwhelmed to think. She didn't want to consider how she felt or what had happened. She didn't want to think at all.

A few moments passed, although Althea had no way of telling the time. The room was dark, a pale swath of moonlight slicing the floor in half.

She heard the steady tread of Demos's footsteps. He came in and turned on a lamp, creating a small circle of light. Then he placed a mug on the table by her head before sitting on the edge of the bed. Waiting.

They remained like that, silent, expectant, for a few moments, with Althea still curled on her side and Demos sitting at the foot of the bed.

Althea eased herself up and took a sip of the drink; it was hot milk. 'Thank you,' she murmured. Demos didn't reply. His shoulders were set rigidly, his jaw tense. He was waiting to hear what had happened. What she had to say. Confess.

Demos deserved it, demanded it, and she found she wanted to be honest. She needed to.

'I told you,' she began slowly, haltingly, 'my mother died when I was thirteen. I loved her, of course, but I wasn't especially close to her. Looking back, I suspect she was unhappy in her marriage.' Her hands cradled the mug, drew warmth from it. 'When she died, in a car accident, my father was devastated. So was I…and it drew us together. I know it might seem strange, but we were happy together then.'

It hurt to remember those few happy months, a gift in the midst of the sorrow and pain of her mother's loss. She could almost feel her hand slipping trustingly into her father's, her head tilting so she could look up at him, see his loving smile. She'd thought he loved her. She'd thought he'd keep her safe.

'He used to take me to the sea every weekend. We'd look for sea glass. We had the most amazing collection.' Her voice hardened briefly, but then she forced herself to continue. 'Anyway, a few months after my mother died, I suppose he realised that we were becoming too reclusive. He was, anyway. He spent more time at work, brought friends—men—home to have dinner with us. I liked it better when it was just the two of us.' She took another fortifying sip of her hot drink, her eyes sliding away from Demos's harsh profile. He said nothing, only waited.

'One of those men,' she said after a moment, her voice careful, precise, 'liked me rather a lot.' She paused, trying to speak through the tightness of her throat, her heart. 'Too much.'

She heard Demos hiss softly. She still couldn't look at him, couldn't see the pity or condemnation that might twist his features. She didn't know which emotion would be there; she could bear neither.

'My father asked me to show him our sea glass collection,' she continued. 'Up in my bedroom.' For a moment she re-membered, relived those moments in her bedroom, the door carefully closed. Moments stolen from her childhood, her innocence. She remembered the hot voice in her ear, murmur-ing, soothing.

*Just be a good girl...*

She closed her eyes, shaking her head against the tide of memory.

She felt Demos's hand on her shoulder, a heavy, comfort-ing weight. 'How long?' he asked quietly.

'Till I was fifteen.' She kept her eyes closed. 'My father sent me to boarding school and it was better then. I only came back on holidays.'

'And when you were fifteen?'

She swallowed. 'He lost interest. I suppose I'd become too grown up. It was as if it had never happened.' She stopped. Demos's hand was still on her shoulder. She couldn't say more. She wouldn't. For this was the hardest, most terrible part to tell.

'And?' Demos asked softly, but Althea shook her head.

'No…'

'There's something more.' His hand tightened briefly on her shoulder. 'What is it, Althea? What else happened?'

'Nothing!' She shrugged off his hand, turning on her side and drawing her knees up to her chest once again. 'Nothing, nothing…' She shook her head—an instinctive, mindless movement. 'Nothing,' she whispered again, and wanted to believe it.

She felt Demos's eyes on her, felt his tension and his judgement. His anger and his disappointment.

*Disappointment.* She swallowed past the tightness in her throat. Surely she had no more tears left to shed? 'Please,' she whispered, 'can't you leave me alone now?'

'No,' Demos replied quietly, 'not yet.'

'I've told you everything!' Her arms crept around her knees, hugging them even more tightly to her chest. 'You know it all now,' she insisted, her voice rising in a helpless cry. 'What more do you want?'

'The truth.' Demos's hands curled over hers, gently stilling her instinctive rocking movements and rolling her onto her back so she was supine before him. Althea gasped at the unrelenting determination lighting his eyes, drawing his face into harsh lines and angles.

'Please… Don't…' She closed her eyes as a single traitorous tear slipped coldly down her cheek. 'Don't make me.'

Demos released her with a sound of self-disgust. 'What do you think I am, Althea? Do you think I'm going to force myself on you like that scum who abused you?'

His voice rang with condemnation and, Althea realised, with hurt. Her throat was dry and aching and she closed her eyes. 'Don't make me *tell*.'

For there was more to tell. The deepest secret she'd held to herself—the secret that now Demos would coldly prise from her.

And she would give it to him, Althea realised, because a part of her wanted him to know. Needed someone else to share the burden of guilt and shame she'd been carrying for so long that it had become a part of herself, as vital as a hand or an eye. She wondered who she would be without its weight. Who she could be. She drew a steadying breath and finally spoke.

'When it—he—stopped, I was relieved.' She kept her eyes squeezed shut; she couldn't look at him. 'Of course I was.' She stopped.

'And?' Demos asked softly.

'And disappointed,' Althea whispered.

*Disappointed.* It was a confession, a revelation of private misery and agonising guilt. She still remembered that streak of confused longing, self-loathing at her own irrational feelings. Demos was silent and Althea kept her eyes closed, unable to face the condemnation and disgust that surely twisted his face.

'What does that make me, to be *disappointed*?' It came out in a tiny, terrible whisper.

He didn't answer, so she answered for him, the fear in her heart finally given an awful and yet liberating voice. She opened her eyes, stared at his expressionless face.

'It makes me,' she said, her voice turning dispassionate, 'exactly the woman you saw in the club. The woman the world sees. The woman in the tabloids. *Worse*.' She'd never spoken that truth, even to herself, had never acknowledged her fear of what she was. What she must be, to feel…

'Is that why?' Demos asked after a moment. His voice was neutral, yet a new understanding dawned bleakly in his eyes. 'Is that why you go to clubs, pretend you're a party girl? Some kind of punishment to yourself?'

'At least then,' she whispered, 'I'm in control. If I *allow* it to happen it's better. And maybe it's who I am.'

'Is it?' Demos's mouth twisted and he gently smoothed a

stray tendril of hair behind her ear. 'It's certainly the image you project, but, no, Althea. It's not who you are. I can testify to that.'

His words echoed emptily through her. 'I'm sorry,' she whispered. 'You married me thinking I was something completely different. I…I thought I was, too. I thought at least I could be what you wanted. Enough.'

Demos was silent for a long moment—long enough for Althea to wonder what he was thinking, feeling. Finally he shrugged. 'We all carry baggage. Regrets. It was unfair and arrogant of me to think you wouldn't have any.' His eyes met hers, and Althea saw a glimmer of tenderness. Gently he reached out and let his fingers skim her cheek, as if he knew that was all the closeness she could bear. 'I'm no psychiatrist, but even I can recognise that conflicting emotions in the kind of situation you experienced would be normal. Expected. You were a child, missing the affection of your father, looking for a replacement, perhaps. Confused, of course, as well, and traumatised. You were bound to be disappointed in some strange way—'

Althea felt a sudden flash of anger. 'Don't psychoanalyse me,' she said. 'I'm not your patient.'

Demos's mouth twisted, cynicism darkening his eyes, and with a terrible jolt Althea realised that that was exactly what she was to him now. His patient. His problem.

And also his wife. She took another breath; she felt exhausted, empty, and yet still she had to ask. She wanted to know. 'And you? What's your baggage, Demos?'

Demos's head was averted, his voice flat. 'I think we'll leave that for another night.'

Althea accepted his answer; she could hardly do otherwise. But she had a suspicion that Demos had no intention of telling her his secrets. His regrets.

Yet he had some. He must have. She thought of the twelve-year-old boy who had shouldered a man's responsibility only to become known as a reckless playboy twenty years later. Why? How?

She thought of Brianna's single word of condemnation:

*Remember*? And she recalled how just a few short hours ago he hadn't defended himself as she'd hit and kicked and hurt.

Why?

What regrets did Demos have? What shadows? And, Althea wondered, would he ever share them with her?

'Did you ever tell your father?' he asked eventually. She didn't reply, and his gaze found hers. 'You did, didn't you? That's why you're so angry with him.'

Her throat was tight, too tight for her to swallow or even to breathe. 'He didn't believe me,' she finally said in a strangled whisper. 'I tried—I *tried*. But he didn't want to hear.' She shook her head. 'I kept telling him I didn't like to be alone with...with *him*.' Even now she didn't want to say the man's name. She didn't like to even think of him. It was, she knew, why she had directed her anger and loathing towards her father. There had been no one else. She understood that much about her own actions, her own heart. 'He was supposed to love me, to keep me safe,' she continued. 'And he didn't. I'll never forgive him for that. I can't.'

Demos didn't answer. Althea pleated the coverlet with her fingers, scarcely able to believe that this man now held all her secrets. She wondered what he would do with them.

A gust of sea breeze rattled the windowpane and then grew still. They had both lapsed into silence—a silence that held its own pall of misery. Althea wished she felt better—wished that she felt the relief of releasing a burden, of having it shared, but she didn't. She was all too conscious of how Demos had taken it on. Yet another burden added to his bowed shoulders, and one he'd never asked for. One that weighed him down.

Another long, aching moment passed, and then he bent and brushed a kiss across her forehead, his lips cool. 'Thank you for telling me,' he said quietly. 'I'll leave you to sleep now.'

He stood, his face angled away from her, and walked from the room. For the first time Althea realised she didn't want him to go.

For the first time she didn't want to be alone.

Yet, she thought despondently as she slid once more beneath the covers, she most certainly was. Perhaps more so than she'd ever been before.

The morning dawned fresh and clear, the sun a bright lemon-yellow above the sparkling sea when Althea awoke. She lay in bed, memories of last night, the words spoken and the tears shed, trickling through her, and with a small ray of surprised hope she realised that she felt better.

Safer.

Stronger.

She'd told, and she'd survived. She was better for it. At least she could be. She could become better. She could heal. She could be strong—not only for herself, but for Demos.

It would take time, patience, courage. And perhaps she had all three. Perhaps, she thought with a flutter of tentative hope, she could have a future…with Demos.

She slid from the bed and padded across the floor to sort through her suitcase of tawdry clothes. She needed new clothes. New clothes for a new person—for a woman who wasn't going to hide behind sexy dresses and sultry smiles. A woman who was determined to be herself…whoever that might prove to be.

A knock sounded on the door and she pushed the discarded clothes aside. 'Come in,' Althea called, and Demos entered. He was showered and dressed, his hair dark and gleaming wet, brushed back from his forehead. He regarded her with those blank silvery eyes, his gaze sweeping the room as if looking for clues. Evidence. Althea felt the uncomfortable prickling of awareness that Demos was treating her like a patient, like someone unsafe. Unstable. And that was not who she wanted to be. That was not who she *would* be.

'I'm looking for clothes,' she said.

Demos arched an eyebrow. 'Don't you have any?'

'I don't want those.'

He gazed at her for a moment, taking in the implications of

that statement before nodding in acceptance. 'We can buy some in town. They won't be particularly fashionable, of course. You'll have to make do with what you have until we can go to the shops.' There was a touch of coolness to his voice.

Althea nodded, strangely stung—hurt—by his tone. His distance. 'Fine.'

Demos nodded back and closed the door once more.

Dressed in jeans and the most modest T-shirt she possessed, Althea met him downstairs. 'What are we doing today? I hope we're not going somewhere fancy.'

'No, nothing like that,' he replied. 'I thought we'd take a walk around the island, see some of the sights.'

They breakfasted on strong coffee and yoghurt with honey, and then, with the sun shining hotly above them, and a light, warm breeze rustling the branches of the oak trees, they set off.

Instead of following the narrow street back down to the harbour Demos took another side street, also steep and narrow, to the right. It wound through the hills between high stone walls before suddenly opening out onto an ancient paved road, now clearly used as a footpath, with the island's hills and valleys spread before them in a living map.

Althea gazed at the terraced green fields, each one enclosed by crumbling stone walls. In the distance she saw a cluster of whitewashed buildings balanced precariously on a mountain-top, as if the houses might slide right off into the sea.

'Ioulida,' Demos said, following her gaze. 'We'll walk there, and on the way we'll see the Lion of Kea—the island's guardian.'

They set off along the road: an ancient, unchanged thorough-fare, of paving stones shaded by olive and fig trees.

'It's very green,' she remarked after they'd walked in com-panionable silence for nearly half an hour. Wild flowers grew determinedly in every crevice and nook in the stone walls and roads, and the rolling fields were lush with new grass.

'Because of the winter rains,' Demos replied. 'Come July it will be as brown and dry as any other island.'

Althea nodded, and felt a tiny shiver of apprehension at his words—as if he was speaking about more than a few colourful weeds. Things could change so quickly, she reminded herself. The day was pleasant, the sun was warm, but it was fleeting. Everything was fleeting.

She sneaked a glance at Demos. His stride was easy, but there was a set to his shoulders, to his mouth, that Althea wasn't sure she liked. She wanted to ask what he was thinking, but she didn't think she really wanted to know.

'What made you buy a villa here?' she asked instead. 'I would have thought you'd prefer Mykonos or Santorini, with their nightlife…'

Demos gave her a quick, hard smile. 'It seems you know me as little as I knew you.'

That remark, made with a dispassionate calm, pierced the bubble of cautious optimism Althea had been insulating herself with. She stopped and turned to face Demos, who reluctantly slowed his stride.

'Then tell me.'

Demos chose to misunderstand. 'I bought a villa here because I wanted to *escape* the crowds, the clubs,' he said with a shrug. 'Somewhere quiet and safe, where I could bring my family. Though that never happened.'

'You mean Brianna?' Althea clarified, and Demos shrugged again.

They continued walking just as a flock of linnets rose from an almond tree fuzzy with pink budding blooms, twittering furiously.

'Did you ever bring Brianna here?' she asked eventually. 'And your mother?'

Demos's mouth tightened, but when he spoke his voice was bland. 'My mother married Stavros,' he replied. 'They made their life together in Piraeus.' It was answer enough; it was all the answer he was going to give.

'Do Brianna and Stavros get along?' Althea asked, and Demos shrugged.

'Well enough.' He paused. 'But she never saw him as her father.'

*No, because that's what you are to her,* Althea filled in silently.

They continued to walk in silence. The footpath wove through the terraced fields before finally opening onto a rocky plateau. Lying gracefully in the middle of it was a huge carved lion.

He was as tall as Althea, weathered and ancient, his paws beginning to crumble. 'Who carved him?' Althea asked, stroking his massive head.

'Who knows? Some ancient optimist.' Demos smiled faintly, his hands shoved in his pockets as he studied the huge beast.

It took Althea a second to see what Demos meant. 'He's smiling!' Now that she saw, she wondered how she could have missed it. The lion was sporting a huge goofy grin.

'That's nice,' she said, tracing her fingers along his wide smile. 'It's as if he's watching over the island. Enjoying it.'

'Yes, it is nice,' Demos murmured, coming to stand behind her. For a moment they seemed united by the shared sentiment, the simple joy in the statue's smile. Althea felt Demos at her shoulder, felt his warmth, and it gave her a sudden ridiculous surge of hope.

Hope.

And love.

The thought was incredible in its novelty. She'd never considered herself capable of love; she'd never looked for it. She'd avoided men, avoided commitment, avoided honesty and caring and truth itself. Because they were all too difficult to bear.

She couldn't trust herself to love a good man; she couldn't trust herself to love at all.

Yet now she found herself wondering if, in the midst of this ill-conceived union, something deeper and more wonderful could be born.

*Love*.

Could she love Demos?

Just as her mind wrapped itself around that intriguing thought, another less welcome one followed.

Whether or not she could love Demos, he would never love her. She remembered his cynical smile the day he'd asked her to marry him.

*I believe in love. I've just had enough of it.*

She understood that now. He'd been stifled by the love and need of his family, of Brianna, by love's burden and responsibility.

The last person Demos would want to love was someone like her, someone complicated and broken. Even if she was mending inside. Healing.

He'd wanted someone sophisticated, sexy and simple. She was none of the above.

And he hadn't even wanted to love her in the first place, when he'd believed her to be all of those things. He could never love her now, knowing who she was. Knowing her secrets. Her weaknesses.

Althea dropped her hand from the stone lion, dispirited. Lions didn't smile. They crouched and pounced and tore you to shreds. She wondered who had possessed such naive hope as to think that a lion might smile, to carve such an impossible creature, believing it might gaze benevolently upon the world.

They had lunch in a small ouzerie in Ioulida, the mountain village, with its narrow arched streets and whitewashed houses. It was, Althea reflected, like stepping back in time; goats ambled along the cobbled streets, and a woman dressed all in black with shiny red cheeks served them with a toothless smile.

The next few days passed with pleasant regularity. Demos took her around the island, showing her the sights: the wreck of the *Britannic*—the sister ship of the *Titanic*, that had inexplicably exploded off the coast road from Korissia—the art museums in Ioulis, the ancient ruins of Carthea.

They bought clothes for her in Ioulis that she liked: plain, simple outfits, clothes she could live in. Be herself in.

And all the while Demos acted like a tour guide, a kindly friend, and she was lulled into the belief—the hope—that she'd first nourished when she had agreed to his proposal. That he would leave her alone and they would both be content to live their separate lives—amicable, apart.

Yet even as she considered that possibility she realised it disappointed her. Already she wanted more from Demos, more than she feared he was willing to give.

She wanted love.

At least, Althea amended, she wanted to see if it was possible. Could she love Demos? Could she love at all?

And could he love her?

'It's too cool to swim,' Demos said one afternoon several days after they'd arrived, 'but we could go to a beach. There's a private one near the villa.'

Althea agreed, and Demos led her to an intimate curve of sand hidden from the town's harbour by an outcropping of rocks. The sea lapped the shore with gentle shushing waves, and a few scattered rocks allowed the sun to warm the tide pools they created.

Curious, Althea slipped off her shoes and rolled up her jeans, dipping her feet into one of the shallow tide pools.

'Be careful,' Demos warned, watching her with his hands in his pockets. 'Those sea anemones can sting.'

Althea glanced down at the fleshy, flower-like creatures, their bright orange tentacles waving lazily in the water. 'I'll be careful,' she promised with a quick smile, and bent down to pick up a mussel shell.

Demos joined her by the shore. 'What are you doing?' he asked in a voice of lazy amusement. Althea ran one finger along the smooth bluish shell. 'Just looking.'

'When you were on that ship,' Demos guessed, 'did you become interested in shells?'

'Marine biology,' Althea admitted with a little self-conscious laugh. 'It's just a hobby, really.' She'd never allowed herself to dream of anything more. She returned the shell to the pool and picked up another one, spiral-shaped and purple, with long, rounded thorns. 'Did you know this shell was used to dye cloth in the ancient world? The imperial purple—but it smelled terribly when you boiled it.'

'Did it?' Demos murmured. He took the shell from her, testing the point of a thorn with one finger. 'How come you left that research ship? You must have been happy there.'

Althea felt a prickle of alarm and she shrugged. 'I told you...'

'Was there a man?' Demo asked abruptly, and she stilled.

'No.'

His gaze swept over her, assessing, knowing. 'Yes,' he said. 'There was.' His eyes bored into hers, demanding answers. 'What happened?'

Althea lifted her chin. If he wanted answers, then fine—he could have them. 'The captain of the ship was a mentor to me—' she began, only to have Demos interject.

'Another father figure?'

'Don't treat me like a patient, Demos,' Althea warned. 'Don't try to analyse me and explain me away. I'm not your sister.' He shrugged, and she continued, 'He became affectionate—hugs, squeezes—it was probably innocent.'

'Probably,' Demos muttered with scathing doubt.

She ignored him. 'I got scared. I scared myself. I realised I couldn't tell what men wanted—whether they were good or bad. I never felt safe. So I left.' She paused. 'I hid.'

Demos was silent for a moment, his expression shuttered. 'And that's why you never finished school?' he asked finally.

She felt a prickle of irritation at his questions. He was trying to understand her, as if she were a puzzle or problem, and yet he refused to allow her the same liberty. 'Actually, I did,' she replied tartly. 'I received my Bacc through an online correspondence course.'

'You did?'

Althea heard the surprised disbelief in Demos's voice and smiled sardonically. 'Yes, I haven't been completely useless these last four years.'

'But why don't you go to university? Get a decent job?'

He made it sound so simple, Althea thought with a hint of bitterness. He'd done it; why couldn't she? She didn't feel like explaining that she'd been afraid, that she felt she'd lost the ability to judge men, to judge herself. That it had been easier to hide, to pretend.

She lifted her chin, hands on her hips. 'Why,' she retorted, 'don't you stop asking me all these questions? I made my choices, Demos. I accept them. Maybe you need to accept yours.'

Demos's brows pulled together in a dark frown. 'What are you talking about?'

Althea took a breath. 'You obviously feel guilty about something,' she said. 'I could see it in the way you talked to Brianna. What happened to make you feel so burdened by her? As if you owe her a debt? From here it looks like she owes *you* one.'

'You know nothing about it.'

'Then tell me,' Althea said, and heard the urgency, the need in her own voice. 'Tell me so I can understand. I gave you my secrets—let me have yours.'

Demos was silent for a long moment—long enough for Althea to wonder. To hope. Then he shook his head. 'I've told you everything you need to know.'

'Don't I need to know more, Demos?' Althea protested. 'I'm your wife.'

'Maybe we need to be husband and wife in every sense of the word to make this work, to move forward,' he murmured, his tone turning lazily speculative.

'Maybe,' Althea replied with asperity, 'we just need to be honest.'

Demos's eyes glittered with intent. 'Then let's be honest with our bodies first.'

She gave a short, hollow laugh, even as her heart-rate kicked up a gear. 'Oh, that will work.' Sex wouldn't solve anything, she knew. It was likely to make things worse.

'Do you ever plan on giving yourself to me, Althea?' Demos

asked quietly. 'You have been with other men, haven't you? As an adult?'

Althea gazed out at the shimmering surface of the sea, blue-green and dancing with sunlight. 'Yes, I have,' she replied after a moment. 'But I never enjoyed it.'

'I'm not surprised.' He moved to stand behind her, laying one hand on her shoulder. It was a gentle touch, yet Althea felt its firm, purposeful heaviness. She knew what Demos wanted. And she almost—almost—wanted to give it to him. 'If Angelos is any indication of the men you've been with, I would hardly expect it to be a pleasant experience.'

'I never slept with Angelos.' She shrugged off his hand and picked her way across the rock-strewn tide pools, looking determinedly for another shell. 'I haven't been with a man in years, actually. I tried at first. I thought it might help. If I were in control, if I *chose*...' She shook her head, refusing to allow the flood of painful memories to wash over her. 'It didn't work, so I stopped.'

'Yet you continued going out, acting like the kind of—?'

Althea cut him off. 'Because that *did* work. The only times I felt out of control were when I hid myself. Do you know what I looked like when I was twelve? Masses of hair and stick-thin legs, miles from puberty or being a woman. Yet I attracted attention. On the boat, I dressed and acted in the least provocative way possible, and yet still...' She shook her head. 'No, the way I've stayed safe is by flaunting myself. And then, ironically, by marrying you.'

'You are safe marrying me,' Demos said in a low voice.

'Safe from every man,' Althea replied, 'but one.'

Demos crossed to her, taking her shoulders to turn her to face him. 'You are safe with me, Althea,' he told her. 'You may have thought you were in control before. You may have felt in control. But you weren't. You were abused and used—nothing more—and it will not be like that between us.'

Althea said nothing. She gazed up at him. His eyes were dark and determined with ferocious intent, and she realised she wanted to believe it. She wanted to know intimacy—love even—and enjoy it. She wanted the touch of another human being, the sweet piercing pleasure of loving and being loved. She was tired of being alone, afraid, apart.

It just seemed so impossible. So unreal.

And Demos wasn't even talking about *love*.

The sun was beginning to sink towards the sea, sending long golden rays of light across its surface. 'It can be good between us, Althea,' Demos continued, his voice filled with gentle yet unyielding promise, 'and it will be...tonight.'

# CHAPTER NINE

THE sun had set, and the first stars glimmered near the horizon as Althea paced her bedroom, her nerves jangling and jumping through her, panic and anticipation warring within her.

Demos had been unshakeable about his promise, his plan. Tonight. He wanted her tonight.

And she wanted to be wanted. She wanted to be loved, touched, treasured—she wanted to discover if it could be as Demos had promised her it could. It was why she had agreed, why she was here, waiting like some archaic virgin sacrifice.

Except she wasn't a virgin. Her mouth twisted in a cynical smile. When she'd agreed to marry Demos she'd believed she could give him what he wanted. What all men wanted… A still, willing body underneath them.

Yet Demos had shown he wanted more than that from her, and she didn't know how to give it. She didn't know if she could.

Yet still she wanted to find out. She would…tonight.

There was a light knock on her door, and then, before she could say a word, Demos entered.

He stood on the threshold, dressed in a white button-down shirt, open at the throat, and a pair of faded chinos. He looked clean and relaxed and, Althea realised, swallowing dryly, utterly appealing.

He moved into the room and Althea saw he was carrying a bottle of wine and two glasses.

'Are you going to get me drunk?' she asked, wiping her damp palms along the sides of her jeans. She hadn't bothered to dress for this encounter; she wasn't going to buckle herself into the kinky scrap of material Iolanthe seemed to think was sleepwear, and there was nothing else appropriate in her suitcase.

'Absolutely not.' Demos set the bottle and glasses on a small table by the window and took a corkscrew from his pocket. 'But a glass or two will help you relax, don't you think?'

'Maybe,' Althea acknowledged, although at this point she didn't think a magnum of champagne would help her to relax. It might make her pass out—which could be preferable.

'I intend this to be enjoyable, Althea,' Demos said, and there was gentle amusement as well as a slight note of censure in his voice.

'Enjoyable for you,' Althea muttered, and he shook his head, handing her a glass of wine.

'No, enjoyable for both of us. This isn't the Dark Ages. Women are allowed to enjoy sex, and certainly what happens between a husband and wife—'

'Is still just sex.' Althea cut him off before taking sip of wine. 'After all, we don't love each other.'

'No,' Demos agreed thoughtfully, also taking a sip, 'we don't.' He gazed out of the window at the night sky. The gentle shush of the sea caressing the shore was audible in the distance. 'Is that what you want?' he asked eventually.

Althea's fingers tightened on the stem of her wine glass. 'You've made it rather clear you don't want to love me,' she replied. 'You said you'd had enough of love.'

'So I did.'

'Do you think…?' Althea paused, swallowed, and started again. 'Do you think that might ever change?'

Demos's face was averted from hers, so she couldn't tell what he was thinking. She could still feel the tension, taut as a wire, stretching between them. 'I don't know,' he said finally. 'But that's hardly something that can be determined tonight.'

He swivelled to face her, and Althea saw a purposeful bland-ness, blankness, in his face. His eyes.

He wasn't very different from other men, she realised with a sharp stab of disappointment. Gentler—kinder, perhaps, when he chose to be. But in the end all he wanted—all any man wanted—was her body. She opened her mouth to tell him so, but then closed it again. What was the point? She was married to this man, and he had a right to expect her willingness. Even if she didn't want to give it.

And even as she acknowledged this, she also realised that she did want to give him her body, her very self. It was a gift born out of…what? Love?

Hope?

'I can see every emotion in your eyes,' Demos murmured. He moved to her, plucking the wine glass from her fingers. 'I wonder how I didn't before. I must have been blind.'

'What am I thinking, then?' Althea challenged.

'You're thinking I'm just like all the others, like any man who uses a woman. But I swear to you, Althea, it won't be like that between us.'

'How can it not be?' she whispered.

'Because you'll be in control.' He smiled at her look of patent disbelief. 'We'll take it slowly, as slowly as you want. As you choose. God knows it'll be an exercise in self-control for me. Now…' his voice deepened with purpose '…we begin.'

Althea tensed and Demos smiled. 'Let's lie down on the bed.' His fingers laced with hers and she followed him woodenly to lie supine on top of the coverlet. Demos stretched out next to her, one arm curved over her head, the other free to roam and touch. He looked relaxed, confident.

In control.

Wasn't she the one who was supposed to be in control? Althea wondered. She already felt as if she were spinning out of it. Had relinquished it the moment she lay here, ripe for the taking.

Carefully Demos laid a hand on her abdomen; underneath his touch her muscles jerked. He rested his hand there, smiling faintly.

'How does this feel?'

*Scary*, she wanted to say, even as she felt a surprising flicker of something—not quite pleasure—at his touch. It wasn't even a caress; he didn't move his hand, and Althea realised he wasn't going to move it any further without her permission. She took a breath. 'Fine.'

He stretched out his fingers, his thumb grazing the bottom of her breast. She tensed.

'And this?'

'You're making me nervous,' she admitted.

'All right.' He pulled his fingers back together, and she let out a shaky laugh.

'This is going to take all night.'

'We have all night.'

She pictured the hours crawling by while she granted him access to her body, inch by torturous inch. 'I'd rather get it over with quickly.'

Demos smiled. 'I know you would. But I'm not going to let you make love to me with just your body, Althea. I want your mind. Your soul. All of you.'

'That's a lot to ask,' she whispered, and she wondered why he wanted it so much.

He smiled. 'I know.'

She realised he'd stretched out his fingers again, and his thumb was once more brushing her breast. She felt a tiny bud of pleasure unfurl within her and took another breath.

'Of course,' Demos continued musingly, 'you could touch me, too.'

'I don't know how.'

'We'll start small.' He reached for the hand lying by her side and gently uncurled her fist, to lay it flat on his chest. She felt his heart beating strongly underneath her palm, felt the smooth, hard contours of his muscles. It was, she reflected, not a bad feeling.

Actually, she decided, stretching her own fingers, it was rather nice. Carefully she brought her other hand up and placed it on his chest. Demos smiled.

His fingers gently stroked her breast through her shirt, sending little ripples of pleasure through her. It was nice, Althea decided, her mind starting to turn hazy, but she'd still be happy to stop.

Her hands tensed on his chest and she glanced up at him, saw his languorous smile even though there was serious intent in his eyes. 'What if I told you to stop now?'

Demos's hands stilled. 'Then I would.'

She took another breath. 'What if I asked you to leave?'

He glanced down at her, his eyes dark, searching. 'Do you want me to?'

Althea paused, considering, and then said, half in surprise, 'No.'

'Do you want me to continue what I was doing?' His hand was still, waiting.

'Yes,' Althea whispered, 'I think I do.'

Demos's fingers touched her again. His thumb grazed over the fullness of her breast, causing a deep shaft of pleasure to pierce her, making her gasp with the strength and purity of sensation. Her own fingers clenched on the buttons of his shirt, and she realised she wanted to touch him. Touch his skin. She'd never wanted to touch anyone before.

'Would you like to take my shirt off?' he murmured, and it amazed her that he knew what she was thinking. Wanting.

'Maybe,' she replied, and when he smiled, waiting, she amended, 'Yes.' He stretched out so she could access the buttons, smiling faintly as she reached for them. Her fingers trembled as she undid each one; she'd done this before, on their wedding night, but it felt so different now. Everything was happening so much more slowly, and yet even so she felt a deep, rising urgency to her movements, to her feelings.

Demos shrugged out of his shirt and Althea gazed at his chest, touched the scar low on his belly, and smiled. 'Knife-fight, huh?'

'I took on six men by myself.'

'I bet you could.' Then, with a new courage she'd never thought to possess, she reached down to kiss the scar, let her lips slide along the silky seared skin, and she heard Demos give a little gasp.

'That feels good.'

She raised her head and met his eyes. 'I'm still afraid.'

Demos nodded and tucked a tendril of hair behind her ear, his fingers skimming her cheek. 'That's all right. We're still going slowly.' He arched one eyebrow. 'In fact, I'm the only one with some clothes off.'

'True,' Althea murmured, and Demos's hand slid under her shirt, rested on her navel. His palm was warm on her skin.

'Maybe we should remedy that situation.'

He'd seen her before, she knew. Even the first night of their acquaintance she'd been wearing less. Yet still she hesitated. This felt so different, so strange and new, so...wonderful.

Wonderful. It amazed her that she could feel this way, that Demos could make her feel this way. Even though the wonder was tinted, tainted, by just a little fear.

'All right,' she whispered. 'But I'll do it.'

Demos nodded and lay back. Althea's fingers trembled only a little bit as she began to undo the buttons of her own shirt. She saw his eyes darken, but the evidence of desire didn't scare her now. It strengthened her. Not with the false illusion of power, but with a heady new sense of what would happen between them, how it could be.

Wonderful.

The buttons undone, she paused for only a second before shrugging her own shirt off. 'There.'

She wore a white cotton bra bought in town, simple and plain. She didn't have generous curves, and she was conscious of it now, smiling uncertainly as his eyes swept over her.

'You look lovely,' Demos told her. He tugged gently on her hand and she lay down again, his hand coming once more to rest on her navel.

They'd got this far, Althea told herself. Lying down, their shirts off—and how much time had passed? An hour? She let out a shaky laugh. 'You're being very patient.'

'It's worth it.'

'How can you be so sure?'

Demos had resumed stroking her—soft, drifting movements that relaxed her even as she felt dizzy with desire. *Desire*. Want, need, pleasure. She could hardly believe the new sensations swimming through her, flooding her senses.

'I know,' he said. 'There was something between us from the moment we first laid eyes on each other. And it's coming to fruition now.'

'Is it?' she whispered, and let out a little choked cry as he lowered his head and his mouth teased her through the thin cotton of her bra. It felt so intimate, so strange. It felt good. Demos lifted his head, his eyes glittering into hers.

'Is that all right?'

'*Yes...*' she choked out as he bent to his ministrations again, and she closed her eyes, her fingers threaded through his hair.

She wanted to touch him again, she realised hazily. She wanted to touch him as he was touching her. Deeply, lovingly.

She'd never wanted that before, had never even thought of it. 'Let me...' she began, and Demos stilled, waited. 'I want to touch you,' she whispered, and he rolled over, taking her with him.

'I've been waiting to hear you say that.'

She was lying half on top of him, and it felt strange—his hardness under her softness, his body supine. Vulnerable.

She ran her fingers lightly down his chest and then bent her head and kissed his chest, the soft hair tickling her lips. Demos groaned, and the sound thrilled her.

Althea kissed him again, touching his skin with her tongue, tasting the faint tang of salt, of man. Empowered by his little groan of pleasure, she moved her mouth lower, and her fingers hovered over his belt buckle.

She lifted her head, and Demos gazed down at her, smiling his eyebrows raised. Waiting.

Althea slid the belt from its buckle and then hesitated. This was starting to get scary.

'What if I do the rest?' Demos murmured, and she nodded her hair swinging down to hide her face.

She watched from behind the curtain of her hair as he undid the rest of his belt and buttons and slid the trousers from his legs. Then his boxer shorts followed and she gave a little gasp

'I didn't mean—'

'I know,' he said with a little chuckle. 'But I thought I might as well.' He arched one eyebrow. 'Should I put them back on?'

Althea took a deep breath and steeled herself to gaze at him—all of him. He was beautiful. 'No,' she said after a moment. 'It's all right.'

'What if you take the rest of your clothes off too?' Demos suggested, and Althea bit her lip.

'We're moving kind of fast here.'

Demos chuckled again. 'I have to confess it feels pretty slow at this end. But all right—keep them on.' He paused. 'For now.'

Althea swallowed, hearing his intent. She might be in control, but at that moment it felt like an illusion. Demos intended this evening to have only one outcome.

'Althea…?' he queried softly, and she tried to smile. 'Don't be afraid.' He stretched out on the bed, naked, unashamed.

Althea's gaze swept over him, all lean, brown sinewy muscle, and swallowed. Desire leapt once more to life within her, a pulsing flame that licked at her insides. 'Maybe I will take them off,' she whispered.

'May I help?'

Her breath hitched as she considered this new and not entirely unwelcome possibility.

Demos grinned in response, his eyes turning silver, and she leaned back as he unbuttoned the top of her jeans and slowly drew the zipper down, his fingers barely brushing her skin. She tensed, expecting to feel exposed, examined, yet under his caressing gaze she found she felt neither.

His eyes cherished her, so she felt like a treasure. She'd never felt like that before, and it made her feel warmed, as if his gaze were sunlight. She lay down as he gently tugged her jeans down her legs and dropped them onto the floor. Her underwear quickly followed, the garments slipping off all too easily.

She was naked.

Demos didn't touch her; he just looked. Althea felt his gaze sweep over her, assessing every curve and swell, and her eyes closed of their own accord. Her body tensed again, memories swimming to the surface as the tide of desire retreated. The evening air was cool on her skin.

'No, don't.' Demos touched her eyes and she opened them, forced herself to look at him. 'We're not,' he reminded her, 'going to do anything you don't want to do.'

'I want to stop,' she blurted, and waited for his reaction. Disappointment. Denial.

Fury.

Yet after a moment of silence, Demos smiled and stretched out next to her.

'What if we pause?' he suggested, his hand still resting with light yet firm possession on the bare skin of her belly.

Althea glanced at him—the sculpted muscle, the evidence of his desire—and smiled ruefully. 'I'm making this rather hard for you.'

'An appropriate choice of words,' Demos agreed with a wry grimace, and she swallowed a surprised laugh.

They lay there quietly, the shushing of the waves and their own breathing the only sounds in the dimly lit room. Gradually Althea felt the panic and fear recede, and she realised he really wasn't going to touch her unless she gave him permission. He'd really meant it when he said she'd be in control. Slowly she began to relax, let her muscles and her mind loosen.

She laid her hand on Demos's chest once more, felt the

crisp hair and hard muscle, the steady beating of his heart under her palm.

He wrapped his fingers around her hand, keeping them there, against his heart.

'Ready?' he asked, and she nodded. He brought her hand to his lips and nibbled the tips of her fingers gently, his other hand stroking her navel. Then longer strokes to take in her breast, the joining of her thighs, his fingers barely brushing those sensitive places before they moved on, sweeping, searching.

She shuddered.

'Was that a good sound?' Demos asked, and she heard the amusement in his voice, the pleasure in the knowledge that he was pleasing her.

'Yes,' she whispered, and let out a little moan as his fingers swept over her once more. She wanted more.

*More.*

She'd never wanted that before.

Her hands swept over the planes of his chest, bunched on his muscles as his own fingers continued to seek her…and found her.

She gasped as he touched her in the hidden heart of herself, gasped again as he stroked her. And then he stopped.

'Good?' he asked, and she could only nod.

He stroked her again, and again, and she moved under his touch, amazed and overwhelmed by the sensations he stirred within her, by the very fact that she could feel them and not be afraid.

She was safe.

Safe here, naked in Demos's arms, with her whole body and heart open to him.

She'd never expected this. She'd never thought to hope for this.

Hope. *Hope.*

Tears sparkled in her eyes and she didn't bother blinking them back. They slipped down her cheeks and she let them, wanted them. These were good tears. They were healing tears.

Demos lifted his hand, reaching to catch a tear with his

thumb. He lowered his head and kissed her on the lips. It was a promise, a gift.

With that kiss Althea knew she would be safe. Always.

'All right?' Demos murmured, stilling once more, and Althea nodded.

'You don't need to ask any more,' she whispered, and he smiled, kissing her again, deeply, with a possession that sealed her soul to his. She didn't want to be in control any more; she didn't want this to be about control, power, authority. She wanted to give those up, to relinquish them with a freedom born of safety, of healing. She wanted to lose herself in sensation and pleasure, only to be found again.

To finally find herself.

And she did find herself. Those scattered and lost pieces were united in a healing whole as Demos moved over her, inside her, filling her body and her heart, her mind and her soul, to overflowing. She cried out and he captured her mouth in a kiss, sealing her heart to his once more.

For now. For ever.

It was after midnight when Demos made his way downstairs into the darkened lounge. His feet and chest were bare; he'd pulled on his chinos before leaving Althea, asleep and peaceful in her bed.

Their bed, their marriage bed. Their marriage finally consummated tonight.

He smiled in memory; it had taken a long, pleasurable while to make Althea his, but in the end she'd given herself to him completely, selflessly, opened her heart and mind to him…as he had to her.

For a moment. Only for a moment. He wondered— doubted—if it could ever be anything more.

If he could let it.

Demos poured a measure of Scotch and settled in a chair by the window. The sea was illuminated by a single sliver of moonlight, a finger of silver on its fathomless black surface.

A tiny ray of light, of hope.

He'd never expected this marriage to challenge him; he'd chosen Althea because he'd thought she *wouldn't*. Yet since the day they'd married—only a week ago now—she'd done nothing but. She'd challenged his perceptions, his beliefs, his desires.

He hadn't wanted someone difficult. Damaged. Someone with ghosts, secrets, pain.

His mouth twisted in a rueful smile. How arrogant and stupid of him to think there were people like that—people who didn't have scars, shadows.

He certainly did.

Yet he couldn't share them with Althea—couldn't burden her with his own memories. She had enough of her own, and it was clear that in this union there was only room for one person's pain.

He exhaled impatiently, his body sated yet still restless. He'd hoped by making Althea his tonight some of those memories, shadows, would be banished. And perhaps hers were… Yet his materialised out of the corners of the room, drifting towards him, hands held out in supplication, mocking voices entreating helplessly.

*I needed you, Demos, and you left me. I believed…*

*It's all your fault.*

*Remember?*

Demos thrust his drink away from him, and it clattered onto the table by his elbow. He didn't want to hear those voices, those painful reminders of his own utter failure as a brother, a son, a man.

And now as a husband.

'Demos?'

He didn't know how long he'd been sitting there, or how long Althea had been standing in the doorway, wearing nothing but one of his shirts, her hair tousled, her feet bare.

'I thought you were asleep.' He realised he spoke roughly, felt it in the still seething mass of memories within him, and he saw it in the confusion that marred her features before she shrugged.

'I was. I woke up.' She moved into the room, one hand resting tentatively on the back of a chair. 'Is everything all right?'

'Fine.' He forced himself to look at her, to smile, and when he spoke again it was with genuine emotion. 'Fine.'

Althea took another step into the room and perched on the edge of a chair. Demos stared back out at the sea.

'What happens now?'

'What?' He jerked around, his eyebrows drawing together in a frown.

'Where do we go from here?' Althea asked. There was a surprising steady gleam in her eyes, and Demos recognised it. Determination.

For what?

What did she want now that he would be able to give her? Yet he knew the answer—saw it in her eyes. Yet another person who needed him, trusted him.

Loved him.

He felt his gut clench as a wave of familiar desolation swept over him.

'Demos?' Her voice was soft, filled with gentle yearning, tender uncertainty. He looked away.

'We return to Athens, I suppose,' he replied with a shrug. 'To Piraeus. I have a yacht to design, and you…you'll be able to do what you like.' He knew he sounded indifferent, uncaring, but he didn't know how to stop. He wasn't sure he even wanted to.

Althea was silent for a long moment. 'What I like?' she finally said, her tone musing. '*Anything* I like?'

He glanced at her sharply and pressed his lips together. 'Within reason. I meant maybe you could take a course if you wanted—something in marine biology—' He broke off at her look of disgust. 'What?' he demanded. 'It's more than you've done before, been given before.'

'I don't want to be *given* anything,' Althea replied. 'I'm not a dog, to be thrown a bone.'

'Fine,' Demos snapped. 'What *do* you want, then?' As soon

as the words were out of his mouth he wished he hadn't spoken them. Challenged her. The old Althea might have flinched and evaded the truth, yet this new woman, reborn from the ashes of her old experience, met his eye with a determined smile.

'I'm glad you asked that question.'

Althea rose from the chair, moved towards him with long, purposeful strides. When she reached him she knelt in front of him, her hands resting on his thighs, even now stirring the embers of desire within him.

Demos gazed at her, his body unmoving, his face expressionless, even as her simple touch caused that leap of life—of hope—within him.

'I want a real marriage, Demos, and I'm not talking about what happens in bed. Although…' a ghost of a smile flickered across her features '…that was nice. That was beautiful. And it was better—*more* than anything I could have ever hoped for.' He opened his mouth to speak but she shook her head, pressing two fingers against his lips. 'I'm talking about a partnership. Equal, giving, maybe even loving.'

He opened his mouth again, or tried to, but she just pressed her fingers harder against his lips.

'I know you don't love me, maybe don't even *want* to love me, and I don't love you. At least I don't think I do. I didn't think I was capable of love, which is why I agreed to your terms for this marriage. But now I realise I want more. I want more than safety. More than not feeling pain. I want to feel good. Happy. And I want to see if I can find that with you.' She dropped her fingers from his lips. 'I want to see if you can find that with me.'

Demos stared at her, kneeling between his sprawled thighs, her shoulders thrown back, her face proud, defiant, vulnerable, and felt a sudden, humbling ache of need, a rush of hope. She waited, her heart, her hope in her eyes, and he opened his mouth to speak.

He didn't know what he was going to say.

Then a tinny trill split the air and broke the moment of silent expectation stretching between them. Althea didn't move, didn't stop gazing at him with her whole heart in her eyes, but Demos did. He shrugged her away and rose from the chair.

The phone trilled again; it was his mobile, his private number, and someone was ringing him in the early hours of the morning.

Whoever it was, for whatever reason, it couldn't be good.

Demos grabbed his mobile from the table where he'd discarded it earlier in the day. He glanced at the number on the little luminous screen. It was, he saw, a hospital in Piraeus. As he gazed at that glowing number he knew what it meant, and he realised he'd been waiting for this moment, waiting with a terrible expectation, for eight years. And in that moment any shred of hope he'd still cherished of a life apart, a life with Althea, vanished— as insubstantial as the evening mist on the sea.

He stabbed the talk button with one finger and spoke roughly into the phone. 'What's happened?'

'Demos, it's your mother.' Nerissa's voice sounded thick with tears, and Demos felt an ominous tightening in his gut. He turned away from Althea so she couldn't see his face.

'What's happened to Brianna?'

'Oh, Demos…' She choked on a sob. 'She's tried to kill herself…again.'

# CHAPTER TEN

It was astonishing, Althea reflected, how quickly things could change. Last night had been the most glorious and transforming experience of her life, and yet today, in the bright glare of morning as they sailed back to Piraeus on Demos's yacht, she felt utterly the same. Utterly alone.

Actually, she thought grimly, she felt worse.

Last night she'd laid both her heart and body bare for Demos. She'd been *honest*. She'd spoken and acted with a truth she hadn't acknowledged or felt in years, and it had been tossed back in her face without so much as a *no thank you*.

Demos hadn't said anything.

In the second before his mobile had rung she'd thought she'd seen a flicker of life in his eyes, of love. Of hope.

Then that persistent trill had split the night—split them apart. For Demos had barely spoken a word to her in the endless hours since then.

Brianna had tried to kill herself. That was all Althea knew. When she'd asked for more details, out of concern, Demos had reprimanded her sharply, informing her with cold, cutting precision that it was none of her business.

Althea had opened her mouth to argue, and then realised the complete waste of effort and emotion such a protest would be. It wasn't her business because Demos was determined for it *not* to be her business.

He was drawing away from her—cutting her off, out of his life. And after only one evening's tantalising glimpse into what it could be like with him she couldn't bear it.

Yet she had to. Because at the moment there was no other choice. Brianna was in crisis; their marriage would come second until that was resolved.

Perhaps, Althea wondered distantly, it would always come second. It had come second even when Demos had proposed; why should she think that—or anything—could really change? Last night she'd finally believed she could change, that the memories and ghosts could be banished. For ever.

Perhaps they couldn't. Perhaps some stayed, restless and hungry.

Hunched over the wheel, his eyes on a distant grim horizon, Demos looked haunted by those memories. Hunted.

They arrived back at Mikrolimano just as the yachts and their owners were stirring to life; it seemed a lifetime ago since she'd stepped aboard Demos's boat, uncertain, afraid, hiding from the truth, from Demos, from herself.

Now she watched as he strode along the dock, not even bothering to see if she followed behind him. She'd become irrelevant or, worse, irritating.

Demos took her to his flat on the harbourside. Althea had never been there before, and she gazed around the rooms with their modern furniture, all sleek surfaces and empty spaces, with a disenchanted air. Demos dropped his bag on the floor, splashed water on his face, and made for the door.

Althea took an instinctive step to follow him.

'No,' he said flatly, not looking at her. 'You stay here.'

'Demos—' She stopped at the blank wall of determination that met her gaze. 'Are you going to the hospital?'

He gave a shrug of assent. 'I'm going by myself, Althea. This has nothing to do with you.'

His utter refusal to include her stung. Hurt. Althea took a deep breath. 'Maybe it should have,' she replied evenly. 'I've been—or nearly been—where Brianna is. I never tried to kill myself, but I know what that kind of despair feels like. I could help her—or at least help you understand. I know how she feels…' Althea trailed off, for Demos was looking at her with such a cold, flat expression—an expression of *loathing*—that she physically recoiled. 'What…?' she whispered.

'Yes,' he replied, in a voice so icy and remote he sounded less than a stranger. He sounded like her enemy, and his words were a condemnation. 'I know you do.'

And then he was gone, the door clicking softly shut behind him, and she was alone.

Althea prowled the flat restlessly, her mind and nerves and heart jumping in desperate uncertainty. Outside, the sea shimmered with sunlight and promise, and as she gazed at its dazzling surface she became conscious of one powerful truth.

She was strong.

She had always been strong. Even in her most desperate moments: as a thirteen-year-old, confused, angry, alone, who had found comfort in pain. Even as a twenty-year-old woman, hiding behind masses of hair and shapeless clothes, afraid to be used again. Even as the woman she'd just been, dancing and flirting with desperate abandon, determined to make the world believe she was wild and reckless and free, a woman who didn't care.

Even now.

Especially now, when her heart cried out for Demos to listen, to let her in. To love her.

For there had emerged a second truth, just as powerful: she loved him.

She'd never thought herself capable of love. She'd hidden from it, denied it, been afraid of it. Yet now it was here, inside her, around her, wrapping her in a warm and steady glow of truth, of power.

Of hope.

She was strong, and she loved Demos. If she held onto those two truths, Althea told herself, she could see herself through this. She could see them both through.

Yet first, she knew, with a sudden, startling clarity, she needed to see someone else. The past couldn't be redeemed, but it could be forgiven.

The townhouse in Kifissia looked empty and forlorn. Althea felt as if a pall of sorrow hung over the house. Her family home—a place of bitterness, pain and regret.

She turned the handle quietly and slipped into the foyer. All was silent. It was Saturday. Melina had the day off, and her father should be at home alone.

Althea walked slowly through the downstairs rooms. They were all empty.

Trepidation fluttered briefly within her as she climbed the stairs.

Then she heard a sound from her own bedroom, and she moved to the threshold. Her father sat on her bed, a pile of sea glass in his lap. Their collection.

She'd kept it, even though she'd come to loathe every piece—always the pretext for private journeys to her bedroom, a softly closed door and then a voice, gentle and yet made more menacing by that false promise of kindness.

*Be a good girl for me.*

Althea hadn't realised she'd closed her eyes; she snapped them open now, banishing the memories. Those pieces of sea glass held no pain, no power.

'Hello, Father,' she said softly, and Spiros jerked in surprise.

'Althea…' He turned around, the sea glass still spilled in his lap, a riot of greens, blues and browns. 'I didn't expect…'

'I know.' She moved into the room and picked up a smooth, curved piece of deep, clear blue. 'I always loved those afternoons we had at the beach. We'd spend hours looking for sea glass.' She glanced up at him and saw the shimmer of tears in his eyes. 'Do you remember?'

'I didn't think you remembered,' Spiros replied in a hoarse voice. He cleared his throat and bent his head, concentrating on returning the sea glass to its jar. Each piece clattered painfully in the silence as Althea watched him, and she realised she wasn't angry any more. Only sad. 'I know I've made mistakes with you,' Spiros continued after a long moment, his head still bent. 'I failed you, and I'm not even sure how. Perhaps I was too strict, or maybe even too soft…at different times.' He glanced up at her, and she saw the stark truth in his eyes. He spoke with difficulty. 'I'm sorry.'

'You didn't fail me, Papa.' Althea's fingers closed around the piece of glass, the curved edge biting into her palm. 'I blamed you for something that wasn't your fault.'

'What…?' Spiros trailed off, and Althea saw the shadow of fear in his eyes. He'd never really known, she realised. He'd never understood what had happened all those years ago. She'd been too ashamed to tell him clearly, and her pitiful, desperate attempts hadn't been enough—not when he hadn't wanted to see. To know. It was, she knew, so easy to hide from the truth. She'd blamed him for hiding from it for so long, but she couldn't now. She didn't want to.

Now she wanted to spare him that truth, for she knew he would be pained by it—tormented, even—and yet this was not the time for dissembling. Lying. That time had come and gone.

'Do you remember,' she began slowly, her throat tight and aching, 'when you brought a business friend home?' She swallowed. 'Gregorios Kourikos.' Even now she didn't want to say the man's name. He'd died, she knew, several years ago, when she'd been on the research ship. He was gone. 'You asked me to show him our collection of sea glass.'

'Yes,' Spiros replied slowly, 'I remember. He took a liking to you, I thought.'

Althea nodded slowly. 'Yes,' she said, gazing into her father's troubled face, 'he did. He liked me very much.'

The silence in the room was a painful, palpable thing, and Althea saw confusion blur her father's features, followed by the dawning of a far more terrible understanding.

'Althea—' he began, his voice a hoarse plea.

'I tried to tell you I didn't like him,' Althea said quietly. 'That I was afraid of him.'

'I thought you were just being childish!' Spiros's face was pale, his eyes wide with new horror. 'I thought you missed the times when it was just the two of us—'

'I did.'

Spiros was silent for a long moment, his head bent, face averted. 'Dear God.' He passed a hand over his face and she saw his shoulders shake with soundless misery. 'That's why…' he mumbled, his head still bowed, and she knew he was putting the fractured pieces of her life—their life—together. 'All this time…'

Althea swallowed; her throat was tight. 'Papa, I let that man control and ruin my life for too many years. Don't give him another moment of it, please. It's over now. It's been over for a long time.' Tentatively, tenderly, she laid a hand on his still trembling shoulder; the bones felt frail under her fingers.

He looked up, his face drawn in bleak lines. 'You must hate me,' he said flatly, and she shook her head.

'I tried to. You were the only one available to hate.' She gave a little laugh that was still filled with sorrow. 'Sometimes I think that everything I did was intended as a punishment for you.' She sighed, shaking her head. 'In the end, it only hurt me.'

'And I forced you to marry,' Spiros finished. 'I thought it would help you—settle you—but it must have been the worst punishment of all.'

'I thought it was,' Althea agreed. 'But it's not. At least, I hope it's not.' *Hope*. Still there, hovering, elusive, transcendent.

Spiros glanced up at her. 'Demos? He's good to you?'

Althea thought of how Demos had looked at her before he left for the hospital. The anger, the despair, the hatred. There was a well of emotion inside him, and she didn't know how deep it was or what to do with the overflow. She glanced at her father. His body was bowed under the weight of her confession, yet love still flickered, shone in his eyes. 'Yes,' she said, smiling sadly, 'he is.'

By the time she'd returned to Demos's flat in Piraeus, Althea was emotionally and physically drained. She tensed herself for a confrontation with Demos, but the flat was dark and empty. She stood in the lounge for only a moment before she made a decision.

She wasn't going to wait any longer. She'd spent half of her life in a desperate limbo of feeling, hiding from life, from living, because she was afraid.

She wasn't going to be afraid any more.

She was going to be strong.

She took a taxi to Nikaia General Hospital in the city, and a nurse directed her to Brianna's room.

Halfway down the hallway she heard Demos's voice, coming from behind a half-open door that led to a waiting room. Althea crept closer to the door and listened.

'She's stable now, thank God. But it was close.' His voice took on a ragged edge. 'For a while it was close.'

'You didn't need to come,' a man replied, and Althea recognised the dour voice of Stavros—Nerissa's husband and Demos's stepfather, if he could be called that. She'd met him briefly at her wedding.

'Of course I needed to come!' Demos bit out. 'She's my sister, Stavros, and God knows I stayed away long enough.'

'Brianna has been in my care since she was thirteen,' Stavros replied steadily. 'I have done right by her. I have always taken care of her.'

Demos was silent for a long moment while Althea waited, her body tensed, her mind spinning.

'I know you have,' he said at last, his voice heavy. 'It is I who have failed.'

'You did what was right,' Stavros replied gruffly.

Althea peeked around the doorway and saw the older man lay a heavy hand on Demos's shoulder.

'You were never her father, Demos.'

Demos tensed underneath the weight of that hand; she saw it in every taut line of his body. In one abrupt, savage movement he shrugged off Stavros's hand and stalked to the window, staring out at the grimy view of an endless car park.

'I wasn't her father,' he said, 'but she wanted me to be. I *tried*—'

He turned around, and Althea forgot to move. The breath froze in her lungs as Demos levelled her with a stare so cold she wondered how he'd ever touched her, loved her.

Yet he had. She knew he had. She believed in that.

'Demos…' she whispered. Stavros turned, and distantly Althea heard him mumble some kind of greeting. She made some response—she must have—although she wasn't aware of what she said. She was only conscious of Demos, staring at her with something that was far too close to hatred.

Stavros left, and they were alone. The silence in the room was palpable, heavy, a burden they both bore.

'Why did you come?' Demos asked eventually, his tone one of uninterest.

'Because I'm your wife. Because I care about you…and your family.' He shook his head, although Althea wasn't sure which part he was denying. She dragged a breath into her lungs. 'Demos—'

'No—don't.' He flung out one hand, his eyes icily silver. 'Don't start, Althea. Don't tell me how you love me simply because I showed you passion. Don't tell me you feel safe with me, you trust me. And for the love of God *don't* tell me you need me. Do you think I can't see all that in your eyes?' He swore aloud and she flinched. 'How did I ever think you were anything but what you truly are? You never hid it. You're a lousy actress,' he spat, and turned away in one jerky movement. 'I believed you were easy and uncomplicated because I chose to.' His voice was flat, dead. 'I chose to because I wanted you. And now I've had you.'

A chill of dread crept up her spine, pooled in her stomach. 'What are you saying?'

'I'm done.' Demos raked a hand through his hair before

letting it fall heavily to his side. 'I'm done with you, Althea. I'm done with this marriage, this farce of a marriage, with having you look at me like I can save you when I won't. I can't. I'm *done*!' The last came out in a roar of anguish that caused tears to start in her eyes.

Demos sank into a chair, his hands buried in his hair, his face hidden. His shoulders shook.

Althea stood on the threshold of the room, of their life together, and knew what this moment meant. She knew, and she was not afraid.

'You can be done with saving me,' she said steadily, 'because you never did. *Love* saved me, Demos. Love did. Not you.' She moved to kneel in front of him, as she had only the night before, when she'd held out the possibility of love; now she gave him the truth of it. 'You've been taking care of everyone since you were twelve. Feodore told me, on the yacht. It was a terrible burden for anyone to bear, and certainly a young boy.'

Demos's body stilled, tensed. He didn't speak for a long moment, and when he did his voice was low, muffled. 'I was glad of it. *Glad*.'

'When your mother married Stavros it all became his responsibility,' Althea surmised, feeling her way through his history. The scattered pieces of his puzzle were beginning to fit. 'And you were left with nothing.'

She could imagine it—picture how a traditional man like Stavros would insist on bearing the burdens of his wife's family. And Demos—young, just coming into his manhood and money, with the house, the *home* he'd hoped to provide for, left empty—had had no role at all.

So he'd chosen one for himself…just as she had. The playboy, the profligate. Because pretending you didn't care was so much easier than admitting you did and weren't allowed.

Althea's heart ached. Her hands slid along Demos's sprawled legs, up his taut arms to the hands that still covered his face. She'd hidden from him this way when he'd asked her to marry him. Yet now she wanted no more hiding—not from their own selves or from each other.

She wanted truth. Honesty, even when it hurt. *Love*.

'I love you, Demos.'

'No, you don't.' He spoke flatly, and her fingers curled around his hands.

'Yes, I do. And you love me.'

He laughed abruptly. 'No, I don't. I'm tired of love, Althea. I told you that when I asked you to marry me. You knew what you were getting into, even if I didn't.'

'You're tired of taking care of people,' Althea corrected. 'Of being responsible for Brianna, who needs help and care that you alone cannot give. That's not love, Demos. That's not the love I'm talking about.' She pulled at his hands, prised at his fingers. 'Look at me.'

Demos dropped his hands slowly, his face ravaged by emotion yet his eyes pitiably blank. His lip curled in derision. Even now he was holding himself apart, if only just.

Althea took a deep breath and summoned the last reserves of her courage and strength. 'I'm not Brianna, Demos. I know what she feels like. I've been there. I've felt that kind of despair, and perhaps you have too. But it doesn't control my life. It's not who I am.' She saw scepticism and something else flash in his eyes. 'I've spent years running away from who I am, trying to be someone else to stay safe. But I'm not going to do that any longer. This is who I am. This is me. And I love you.'

She waited, and even though everything was on the line— life, love—she wasn't afraid. She felt sure, strong, certain. She clung to that.

Finally Demos spoke.

'It's not you I doubt,' he said in a low voice. His voice came out in a raw whisper of condemnation, confession. 'It's me.' He drew a ragged breath. 'I've been taking care of Brianna since she was a baby,' he said after a long moment. His gaze was un-focussed, his eyes on a distant memory. 'I told you before. I took care of my family, all of them, but Brianna looked up to me in a way my other sisters didn't. I was proud. I thought I could take care of her…and I didn't.'

Althea waited, the silent *why* on her lips unspoken.

'I left her,' Demos said with a bleak smile. 'I spent twelve years working as hard as I could, earning pennies to provide for them all, and when I'd finally put myself through school there was nothing left for me to do. Stavros had asked my mother to marry him, and he was all they needed. He told me so, and I agreed.' His smile twisted bitterly. 'My mother thought they were releasing me, allowing me the freedom she believed I'd always craved. And of course I *had* craved it. I'd resented them all, Althea, every single one of them, looking at me as if I could rescue them all. As if I were a saviour instead of a man. Just a man. A *boy*.'

He rubbed a weary hand over his face. 'When I realised I was free to pursue my own pleasure, I was relieved.' He glanced at her now, his gaze pleading for understanding. Forgiveness. 'You asked what kind of woman it made you, to have felt disappointment. And I ask the opposite, Althea. What kind of man does it make me, to have been relieved? *Relieved* that I no longer had that burden, had Brianna gazing up at me as if I were her hero? Because of course as a hero I failed spectacularly. Just three months after I walked out of their lives Brianna tried to kill herself.' He reached for her arm, turning it so the pale white scars were visible once more. 'She cut herself up a lot worse than you ever did.'

'That wasn't your fault,' Althea whispered. Tears shimmered in her eyes, and her throat was so tight it hurt to speak. Everything hurt, and yet it needed to. They needed to go through this…together. She only prayed—*hoped*—they'd still be together on the other side.

'Wasn't it?' Demos asked after a moment, his voice turning remote once more. She was losing him—losing him to his guilt and regret. 'She told me it was. Those were her exact words. I think of that every day. If I hadn't gone my own way perhaps she wouldn't have done it. Perhaps I could have saved her—'

'No one can save another person, Demos,' Althea said quietly. 'No one has that responsibility.'

His eyes met hers, dark and unyielding. 'Perhaps not. But do you think that really makes a difference? She begged me to stay. She told me I'd promised. And I had. But I thought it was better for her to be with Stavros, to have a real family. And you know the truth? I wanted to be free. I felt I deserved that.' He shook his head. 'I was selfish, and it almost cost Brianna's life…twice.'

Althea shook her head. 'It wasn't your job to provide a family, Demos.'

'Yes, it was!'

His voice came out in a savage roar and he jerked away from her. But Althea held on, clenching her hands around his so tightly her knuckles were white. Demos didn't let go. She wondered if he was even aware of that desperate hold.

'You know why I wanted to marry someone uncomplicated?' he asked, his tone bitter. 'Someone who seemed sexy and simple, a fun-loving party girl? Oh, I convinced myself it was what I wanted. What I needed. But the truth?' He drew a shattered breath. 'Because I didn't want to fail again.' His gaze met hers, and Althea saw the despair in them. Felt it. 'I didn't want to fail you.'

'You haven't,' she whispered.

'Then it's only a matter of time.'

He was drawing away from her again. She saw it in his eyes as he turned his head away from her, felt it as his hands slid from hers.

'Demos, we're both going to fail each other,' she said, her voice taking on a ragged, desperate edge. 'Look at our wedding night! That was a fiasco, and one we survived. That's life, Demos. That's *love*. You fail and you fail and you disappoint— and you know what? You keep hanging on to each other. You stay. You make it work.'

'I *can't*...' It was no more than a whisper.

'And you know why you make it work?' she continued with fierce determination. 'Because of hope. *Elpis*. Remember?' Her hands curled around his once more, her nails digging into his skin, making him feel, hurt, remember. 'It's true. This is true.'

Demos was silent for another long moment. She felt his hands, his heart resist, and then his fingers curled around hers, held hers, and she felt a leap of hope, a rush of love.

'I was afraid,' he finally said quietly. 'When I realised you had a past—shadows—I was afraid again. I hate that fear. I hate feeling it, knowing I might lose you. Fail you…like I did Brianna.'

'You don't need to be afraid,' Althea whispered. 'Or at least let's be afraid together. I'm terrified right now.' She offered him a shaky smile, and saw the faintest glimmer of a smile in his eyes, his mouth.

'How did you get to be so wise?' he murmured. 'So strong?'

'Love,' Althea replied simply, and she believed it with every fibre of her being.

Outside in the hospital corridor a nurse pushed a trolley with a squeaky wheel, and somewhere a child giggled and fell silent. Muted sounds from a distant world, a world that continued to shift and change even as they remained suspended, separate.

Althea waited.

'I love you,' Demos said finally. 'I love your strength, your courage.' He smiled sadly. 'But it doesn't change anything. It doesn't change who I am, or who you are, or what will happen.' His glance slid to the doorway, as if he could see beyond the room to where Brianna lay in her hospital bed. 'I don't know what will happen. Nothing's changed.'

Althea raised his hands to her lips and kissed the salty skin. 'Actually,' she said, 'it changes everything.'

Another moment passed; how could she endure the waiting, the uncertainty? Then Demos smiled. He brought his hands up to cradle her face and drew her closer to him, to the circle of his arms, where she was safe. Where she belonged.

'Maybe it does,' he murmured, and kissed her with a deep, endless tenderness that came from that well of emotion, its wonderful overflow. 'Maybe it does.'

They remained that way for a long time: Althea kneeling between his thighs, Demos cradling her, her head against his shoulder, the steady, soothing beat of his heart against her cheek.

Here she was home. Here she was safe.

She didn't know what the future held, what help Brianna would need, or even what shape her married life with Demos would take. All was uncertain. And yet in the midst of it was the one, the only truth she needed. Love. Safety.

Hope.

MILLS & BOON

# MODERN

## On sale 6th February 2009

### BOUGHT FOR THE SICILIAN BILLIONAIRE'S BED
*by Sharon Kendrick*

Needing respite from predatory women, billionaire Salvatore Cardini impulsively asked his *cleaner* to be his mistress! Jessica reluctantly agreed, but she hadn't realised her role wasn't merely public – she's his mistress in private, too!

### COUNT MAXIME'S VIRGIN
*by Susan Stephens*

Virgin Tara is seduced by the Count Lucien Maxime, but too late realises that she's been purchased, just like everything around her. She flees, heartbroken. But a tragedy brings them into contact once again and this time the Count won't let her get away...

### THE ITALIAN'S RUTHLESS BABY BARGAIN
*by Margaret Mayo*

Nanny Penny knows working for Santo De Luca will make him hard to resist, and she's right! Inevitably, they have a passionate affair – and then Penny falls pregnant...

### VALENTI'S ONE MONTH MISTRESS
*by Sabrina Phillips*

Years ago, Faye fell for Dante Valenti – but he took her virginity and left her heartbroken. She'd sworn, *Never again!* But what Dante wants, Dante takes...

# 4 FREE

## BOOKS AND A SURPRISE GIFT!

We would like to take this opportunity to thank you for reading this Mills & Boon® book by offering you the chance to take FOUR more specially selected titles from the Modern™ series absolutely FREE! We're also making this offer to introduce you to the benefits of the Mills & Boon® Book Club™—

- ★ FREE home delivery
- ★ FREE gifts and competitions
- ★ FREE monthly Newsletter
- ★ Exclusive Mills & Boon Book Club offers
- ★ Books available before they're in the shops

Accepting these FREE books and gift places you under no obligation to buy, you may cancel at any time, even after receiving your free shipment. Simply complete your details below and return the entire page to the address below. You don't even need a stamp!

**YES!** Please send me 4 free Modern books and a surprise gift. I understand that unless you hear from me, I will receive 6 superb new titles every month for just £2.99 each, postage and packing free. I am under no obligation to purchase any books and may cancel my subscription at any time. The free books and gift will be mine to keep in any case.

P9ZED

Ms/Mrs/Miss/Mr ................................................Initials ......................
BLOCK CAPITALS PLEASE

Surname ............................................................................................

Address ............................................................................................

............................................................................................................

................................................................Postcode................................

**Send this whole page to:**
**UK: FREEPOST CN81, Croydon, CR9 3WZ**